SAVING THE COWBOY'S CHRISTMAS

ROWDY RANCH

Vicki Lewis Thompson

Ocean Dance Press

SAVING THE COWBOY'S CHRISTMAS
© 2024 Vicki Lewis Thompson

ISBN: 978-1-63803-917-4

Ocean Dance Press LLC
PO Box 69901
Oro Valley, AZ 85737

Visit the author's website at
VickiLewisThompson.com

"We need to stop." Rance's gentle murmur caressed Lani's damp lips with a brush of air.

He was calling a halt? That was her job! She wiggled away from him, out of breath and pretending she wasn't. "What's this *we* business? I didn't agree to that kiss. That was all your idea."

"Yes, ma'am."

"And wipe that smug smile off your face. You caught me in a weak moment. I recently... broke up with someone."

"Oh? I'm sorry."

"You don't look sorry."

"Okay, I'm not. I'm the opposite of sorry. But I didn't know you were in a relationship. Did you mention him in August? Because I don't remember anything about—"

"I wasn't involved with him then."

"A short relationship."

"Almost four months!"

"A medium-sized relationship?"

"A significant one. Transformative."

"Uh-huh. Super smart guy. Lousy in the sack."

She fought the urge to laugh. "You could say that."

He tugged on the brim of his hat in a typical Rance gesture. "I believe I just did."

1

"I wish ya luck, luv." Granny Haggerty's brow puckered as she gazed at Rance. "But she'll be knowin' ya tricked her. She'll eat yer head off."

"Probably." When the McLintocks had welcomed Kieran Haggerty and his grandma to Rowdy Ranch back in October, Rance had engineered having Granny temporarily housed in his guest room until her cabin was built.

He had many reasons for it and this was one of them. She gave good advice. And she was solidly against his plan to rope Lani into taking a private sleighride. "But telling her Sara and Kieran were going was the only way—"

"Apart from tellin' her the truth, that you have a special gift for her." Granny crossed her arms over the green checked apron covering her ample chest. A recent perm and a golden blonde dye job made her look like a cherub, especially since a lifetime in Ireland had blessed her with wrinkle-free cheeks. "You'll be startin' off with a lie."

"A little white one. The only lie I've ever told her. I'll confess the minute she questions me."

He took his jacket from the coat rack by the door and shoved his arms into the sleeves.

"Why wait? Tell her straight off they weren't ever plannin' ta go. Admit ya lied and promise never to do it again."

"Hm." He buttoned up and grabbed his Stetson off the rack. A full confession could be a wise move. "Okay, I'll do that."

Granny smiled, her blue gaze warm. "Good on you, boyo."

"I'll be back in time to take you over to the house for tea." He slung a backpack over his shoulder and picked up a festively wrapped package from a table by the door. She'd helped him tie the fancy red bow.

"You'll be back sooner than that if she refuses ta—"

"I doubt she will." He hefted the package. "I'm counting on this."

"'Tis a precious gift, lad." She paused. "Nervous, are you?"

"Like a paratrooper leaping into battle." Bending down, he kissed her cheek.

She flushed and patted his arm. "Go on with ya. I'll be lightin' a candle after ya leave."

"Thank you for that." Picking up his keys, he opened the door and slipped out quickly to minimize the blast of cold air on Granny. She would never know how much he cherished her prayers.

The midday sun had warmed Thunder's cab, but not much. Cold leather chilled his butt. He laid the backpack on the floor and the package on the passenger seat. His stomach felt like he'd eaten a handful of habanero chilis and washed them down with 100-proof tequila.

Two weeks ago, this plan had looked brilliant. At least to him. Sara and Kieran had agreed to help. They could hardly say no when he'd worked so hard to nurture their romance.

But they'd warned him Lani would back out the minute she sensed a trap. That's why Granny's suggestion was a good one. He'd disarm her first thing by explaining he had a top-secret Christmas present he didn't want anyone else to know about.

Nobody except Granny. For almost two months she'd been his muse and accomplice. In exchange, he'd knocked himself out showing his gratitude.

Prior to her arrival with Kieran, he'd scoured antique stores to find a bed that looked like the four-poster she'd left behind. The matching dresser had been a bonus. On impulse, he'd bought a framed watercolor of the Irish countryside.

She'd cried happy tears when he'd shown her into her room, which he'd made up with the linens she'd shipped ahead. She'd also mailed a small collection of framed pictures and knickknacks. He'd unpacked and arranged those, too.

One was a picture of her late daughter, Kieran's mother and Lucky's, as it turned out. That lady's spirit of adventure had been the source of so much pain, and now so much happiness. Including his.

Before making his bid to have Granny stay with him, he'd checked with Lucky and Kieran to make sure he wasn't stepping on toes. Lucky was grateful. His busy schedule with the second bookstore meant he and Oksana would be forced to leave Granny alone in their cabin for days at a time.

Kieran and Sara were bunking in the kids' wing until their cabin was finished. Granny could have done the same, which would have put her close to them. A mite too close, considering without her they'd have the wing to themselves now that the senior Armstrongs were in their new cabin and Lani was staying in their guest room.

Kieran and Sara would never have brought up the privacy issue, but evidently Granny had figured it out because she'd specifically asked to move in with Rance for the time being. Excellent choice. She had her own bathroom and free rein in the kitchen. Her pool game was coming along nicely, too.

Rance arrived at the barn thirty minutes ahead of the time everyone was supposed to meet. That way he could help Buck tack up Thor and hitch him to the sleigh. Yesterday they'd hauled it from the tractor barn to a spot close to the horse barn.

It looked damned good sitting there in the snowy yard. Over Thanksgiving Angie had given it a fresh coat of red paint, touched up the gilt trim and polished the fancy curved runners.

Once the caramel-colored Belgian was hitched to it, the sleigh became something out of a storybook. Just what he had in mind for this encounter with Lani.

As he shut off the engine, Buck came out of the barn leading Thor. The big guy's ears barely cleared the lintel as Buck took him over toward the sleigh.

He was already tacked up, too. So much for helping with that part. It was just like Buck to get a head start, though.

Rance left the package in the truck, along with a small bag of carrot pieces he'd stuck in the backpack. If he left them in the backpack, Thor would smell them and want his treat early.

Grabbing the pack, he climbed out. "Thanks for tacking him up, Buck."

"Happy to." He thumbed back his hat and gave Rance a smile. "I'm glad you're taking him out. He could use a few trips with the sleigh before we trailer him into town for the Christmas Eve gig."

"I've heard they sold a bunch of tickets."

"I bought several myself."

"Me, too. " The Main Street sleigh ride was a popular Wagon Train tradition — fun for all and the proceeds benefitted needy families. If today turned out the way he hoped, Lani would agree to take that ride with him on Christmas Eve.

He deposited the backpack in the sleigh. He'd brought a thermos of hot chocolate and two mugs for when they stopped in the meadow. Theoretically, he'd give her the present at that point.

He and Buck worked well together and they hitched up Thor in a jiffy. That gave him time to explain his plan, mentioning a special gift but not specifying what it was. "So I won't need you to drive, after all," he said. "I'll do it."

Buck's expression was much like Granny's had been. He shook his head. "She's gonna be ticked off at you, son."

"I'm hoping she'll forgive me after she opens my gift."

"Please don't tell me you got her a ring. That would be—"

"Suicide?"

"No kidding! She doesn't even like you all that much, let alone love you."

He was aware of that fact. He turned her on, though, also a fact. Her reluctance to be alone with him proved it. "I'm not giving her a ring. Something better."

"What?"

"I can't tell you yet, but I—" The sound of a truck drew his attention to the road. He'd offered to pick Lani up from her parents' cabin but she'd refused his offer. Instead she was borrowing her folks' new truck.

"That's probably her." If so, she was early. And he hadn't transferred the package to the sleigh.

"That's my cue to head on home and leave you to work this out." Buck laid a hand on his shoulder. "I advise you to tell her right away that you've pulled a fast one."

"I will. Granny said the same thing." The sound of the truck grew louder. Soon it would make the turn and Lani would be able to see him move the package.

Buck grinned. "I'm not surprised. Are you bringing Granny over for tea this afternoon? Marybeth's counting on it."

"I am. Those two really hit it off." Yeah, he'd have to move it with her watching him. Not optimal.

"Yep. I had no idea my wife had such a hankering to reminisce about her summer in Ireland. Okay, I'm off. Give me a call when you come back. It's easier with two of us." He gave Thor's flank an affectionate pat and walked toward the path he'd shoveled after the last snow. He and Marybeth lived a convenient three-minute walk from the barn.

Rance strolled toward his truck just as the Armstrong's school-bus yellow truck appeared in his peripheral vision. Climbing in the driver's side, he tucked the package inside his jacket and left the truck, again maintaining a leisurely pace.

A thick green lap robe was stored in a compartment under the seat of the sleigh. Taking it out, he laid the package on the wooden floor and casually tossed the blanket so it was partly on the seat and partly on the floor.

Lani pulled in on the far side of Thunder. He wouldn't be able to see her climb out.

What if she'd decided to invite her folks at the last minute? That had never occurred to him. It could happen. The sleigh held six.

Heart pumping fast, he waited to see who appeared around Thunder's back bumper. Lani walked toward him. Alone. Thank the Lord.

"Where is everybody?" She glanced around. "Where's Buck? Did you hitch up Thor by yourself?"

"No, I—"

"The sleigh looks great. I'm a little early, but I thought Kieran and Sara would be out here helping. I didn't want to sail in like some princess when all the work was done."

She delivered the words fast, the way she did when she was nervous. The cold air kissed her cheeks and turned them pink while sunlight caressed her hair, teasing out the multiple shades of brown.

Pulling a red knit hat from the pocket of her coat, she tugged it on while looking everywhere but at him. "Should I go up to the house and get them?" She took knit gloves from her other pocket. "I can imagine Sara oversleeping, but Kieran's not the type to—"

"They're not coming."

That got her to look at him, her hazel eyes narrowing. "Why not?"

"Because… they were never supposed to go. I set this up so I could—"

"You ratfink!" She clenched her gloved hands.

He almost laughed. Who said that anymore? "I have a good reason."

"No, you don't." Her cheeks flushed to a deeper pink. "Whatever lamebrained excuse you come up with will never be good enough to justify *this*." She swept a hand toward Thor and the sleigh. "You got me out of bed for nothing. You got this poor horse out of bed for nothing." She spun on her heel.

"Lani, wait."

"No chance." She stormed off toward the yellow truck, her arms swinging at her sides.

He followed her. "I have something for you. It's your favorite thing in the world."

She paused but didn't turn. "That's impossible."

"Is it?" He stopped a few paces away, giving her space.

"You don't even know my favorite thing."

"I do, because you told me."

"I did not."

"Technically you told my mom, but I was there. You said your favorite thing was getting a manuscript from a promising writer. You said it was like opening a present on Christmas morning."

She turned. "You have Oksana's next book?"

"No."

"Then whose?"

"Mine."

2

For a few seconds Lani lost her balance as the world shifted under her feet. Rance wrote a book? Impossible. He wouldn't be able to sit still long enough.

He had to be pranking her. Yeah, that was it. "I can't imagine where you're going with this nutty conversation but count me out." She headed for her parents' truck.

He hurried after her, his long strides catching her easily. "You don't believe me?"

"I do not."

"Wait here. I'll fetch it."

Her pesky curiosity got the better of her. Might as well find out what constituted a book in his mind. She turned around and sure enough, here he came carrying a rectangular package wrapped in festive paper topped with an elaborate velvet bow.

If he'd tied that bow then she was Elmer Fudd. But the box was more than two inches thick. If it contained a manuscript, it wasn't just a few pages. What the hell was he up to?

Stopping in front of her, he paused to catch his breath, his gaze fixed on that elaborate red bow.

An uneasy feeling grew in the pit of her stomach. She could be wrong, but she was picking up an emotion she'd never associated with Rance McLintock. Was he anxious?

He glanced up, a crease between his dark brows. "I realize these days manuscripts are submitted digitally, but you've said the publisher you work for still takes hard copy." He swallowed.

Oh, no. He really *had* written a book. And he was giving it to her. In Christmas wrapping paper with a horse and sleigh motif, no less.

Gone was his jaunty self-confidence. She'd worked with enough first-time authors to appreciate the courage he'd summoned to get through this moment. She'd have to be made of stone not to empathize.

The warm squishy feeling in her chest was just that — empathy. Nothing more. "What kind of book is it?" Maybe it would be non-fiction and she could pass it on to a colleague.

"Fiction." He cleared his throat. "A contemporary Western."

"Oh." Right up her alley. Considering his mom wrote historical Westerns, which he'd been reading all his life, his similar-but-different choice made sense.

"This is the first in a series. There will be a mystery in each book." His voice steadied. "The hero's a former deputy who left law enforcement and bought a bar. He has an Irish granny."

"I see." No wonder he'd wanted Granny to stay with him. Research.

"The heroine's family is Italian and she's the elected sheriff of this small town where the bar's located. She discovers that the bar owner makes a good undercover agent." He was into it, now, a glow of excitement chasing away the last of his anxiety. "Their relationship is something like that old TV show with Bruce Willis and Cybill Shepherd."

"*Moonlighting*?"

"That's the one. Just substitute a small Western town for LA."

"So *Moonlighting*, only with cowboys."

"Yes, ma'am."

Dammit, he'd come up with a viable story concept. She was already writing the blurb in her head, imagining the marketing campaign, seeing potential cover treatments.

But this was Rance, the guy she'd vowed to stay away from. Far, far away. Anyway, she still didn't know if he could write. He was the son of an *NYT* bestseller, but so were all the McLintock kids and nobody else in that bunch had written a book. Oksana, Lucky's wife, was the only other author in the family.

Meeting his gaze, she pretended the sizzle in her veins was professional enthusiasm. "Does your mom know about this?"

"Not yet. Nobody does except Granny. And now you."

"You've written an entire book while living in the midst of this close-knit family and *nobody* knows? Or even suspects?"

"Why would they? When I told you, you didn't believe me."

"Yes, but I'm only a casual visitor. I don't know you as well as they do."

"I can play my cards close to the vest."

"Maybe. To a point, but still."

"It's not as tough as you think. I live alone and have a fair amount of unobserved free time. I give the impression that I spend most of it playing pool."

"That's logical since you're so good at it."

"And shooting pool is also great for working through a tricky plot problem."

Every word out of his mouth strengthened the possibility that he was the real deal. He talked like a writer, a serious writer with a goal and a plan.

But handing the manuscript to her was ridiculous. He was the son of a bestseller. "I appreciate your gesture in offering it to me, but I work for a very small publisher. You need to follow Oksana's lead and get your mom involved. You could end up in a bidding war like she did."

"How do you know? You haven't read the book."

"No, but—"

"I think it's decent or I wouldn't be giving it to you. You're also the only person I trust to give me an honest opinion. Everybody else likes me too much."

That made her laugh. It was so Rance. "Then nobody's laid eyes on it, not even Granny?"

"She's seen snippets, the parts where I needed to check my fictional granny's dialogue, but all along I wanted you to be my first reader."

"All along? When did you start this?"

"Last February, after you went back to New Jersey."

"Please don't say you wrote it for me."

"No, but you were the catalyst. This story's been fermenting for a while. I always knew I'd write it someday. Then I met you and everything fell into place. I'd write the book in secret and hand it to you. You'd tell me whether it's any good."

"But if I think it's publishable, then you should have your mom—"

"I won't ride on her coattails."

His stock just went way up. She held his gaze, captured by the gleam of self-respect in his brown eyes. "I get that."

"Will you take it?" He held out the package.

She hesitated. "Yes." She picked it up, gripping it tight with both hands as her gloved fingers slipped on the wrapping paper.

"Thank you." His deep sigh of relief told her how much he'd counted on this.

"It's heavy."

"Ninety-nine thousand five hundred and sixty-two words."

She smiled. "I would've guessed ninety-nine thousand five hundred and sixty-three."

"In my final pass I cut a word on the last page."

She peered at him. "Seriously?"

"No." He laughed. "I have no idea how many words it is. I kept editing right up to the last minute before I had to print it out. It's slightly under a hundred thousand. I think."

"I feel like I just got the handoff in a spy movie. I assume I'm sworn to secrecy?"

"If you can manage it."

"It'll be tricky. I'll need to read when no one's around. And someone's always around."

"But not on this sleighride."

"That was your plan?"

"No, ma'am. My plan's been banjaxed, as Kieran would say. I'd intended for you to ride shotgun while I drove the sleigh."

"What about the book?"

"I was gonna find a good place to stop and pull it out from under the blanket."

"What made you think I'd agree to go with you?"

"I would've said you could do some of the driving."

She glanced at Thor standing patiently, harnessed up and ready to rumble. "That sounds like fun."

"But now I'm thinking you'd be more comfortable sitting in the sleigh."

"While reading your book."

"It's a thought. Not that you couldn't drive the sleigh at some point. If you want to."

"I do." She was also itching to open the package. But she couldn't do it here and the longer they debated the subject the more likely someone would show up and blow their cover. "Ninety-nine thousand words is a lot. I can't possibly—"

"You'd get far enough to make an evaluation."

"True." Excitement ramped up her heart rate. She lived for this. Every manuscript was a voyage into uncharted territory. No one had been there before her. In this case, literally no one.

On top of that, the unlikely author was a drop-dead gorgeous cowboy. She'd fought her attraction to him for months. If it turned out he could write....

"Shall we go?"

She sucked in a breath. "Yes."

<u>3</u>

Rance wasted no time settling Lani in the sleigh and heading out.

"What's in the backpack?"

"A thermos of hot chocolate and a couple of mugs."

"Can you drink and drive?"

"No, and you probably shouldn't try drinking it while we're moving. Our turnaround point is a pretty little meadow. We can stop there."

"Um, okay."

She was suspicious and he didn't blame her. He'd fantasized kissing her while they were stopped in the meadow. But the mood had to be right. If it wasn't, he'd wait. His time would come.

At least Mother Nature had cooperated with his plan. A recent snowstorm had dropped enough of the white stuff to fill ruts in the ranch roads but not so much they required a plow.

Perfect for a fast getaway. He urged Thor into a trot up his mom's road to the main ranch road. At the juncture he went left, which would take them past his cabin. Maybe Granny would hear the sleighbells and know he'd made it this far into his scheme.

The distinctive jingle and the clippity-clop of Thor's hooves stood out in the silent, wintry morning. The rustle of paper as Lani unwrapped the box stood out, too.

"I'm impressed you found paper with sleighs on it. Nice touch."

"My specialty."

She snorted.

He'd automatically given a cocky response, but despite the cold, he was sweating bullets. What if she didn't like it?

Worse yet, what if she was bored? The book was his emissary. If she was bored with it, she'd be bored with him and all his dreams would die a miserable death.

A soft scrape and pop signaled she'd opened the box, which meant she'd seen his title, *Tequila Shots in the Dark.* "That title can change. I just wanted something bar related."

"I like it."

His breath hitched and a small spark of hope flickered in his heart. "Thanks."

"No pseudonym?"

"Mom gave me a cowboy name so I might as well use it."

"Good choice."

At least she liked his name. So did he, when it came down to it. Rance was Jimmy Stewart's character in *The Man Who Shot Liberty Valance.* Being named after him didn't suck.

He'd visualized *RANCE MCLINTOCK* on the cover and liked the look of it. He'd considered creating a mockup of a Stetson lying on a bar along with a badge and an empty shot glass. But his computer skills for creating images weren't great and he couldn't farm it out since the project was top secret.

He started to tell Lani about his cover concept. Changed his mind when the swish of a page told him she'd moved on. *Button your lip, idiot. Let your book do the talking.*

He was so focused on what was happening behind him that he would have missed the turnoff coming up on his right. Thor didn't. Thanks to the Belgian they left the road and were now moving through the trees.

He'd been part of a family work party a few years ago when they'd cleared a path that was specifically sleigh-friendly. While the sleigh could handle other trails leading directly from the ranch, this one provided a smoother experience with less chance of getting smacked by a branch. The meadow turnaround was handy, too.

On the most important sleigh ride of his life, he wanted the runners to glide like the blades of Olympic figure skaters. Which they did, leaving him free to concentrate on each turn of the page, every intake of breath. The little gasps were precious. He was proud of the suspense he'd created in the first few pages.

When she let out a soft chuckle, he treasured that even more. She was enjoying herself. Bartender Dooley and Sheriff Sophia were keeping her entertained. So far.

Pain in his jaw told him he was clenching his teeth. And tightening every muscle in his body, on top of it. He had a death grip on the lines, totally unnecessary when Thor knew the route and wasn't the least bit skittish.

Time to relax. He loosened his grasp on the lines, gently pulled cold air into his lungs and let it out gradually. He should have brought earplugs. Turning up the thick collar of his jacket didn't block the crackle of flipped pages, the rapid shifts in Lani's breathing or her quick gasps and soft giggles.

Initially he congratulated himself on her laughter. Then paranoia set in. What if she was quietly giggling because the writing was ridiculously bad?

No. No, it wasn't. He'd been trained from the age of two to separate good writing from dreck. He'd had a flair for this from the get-go. He'd aced every writing assignment in high school.

Then again, he loved this story, loved Dooley and Sophia. If love was blind, he wouldn't be able to see their flaws or the plot holes he'd left for them to fall into. He... wait, why weren't they moving?

Oh. They were in the meadow. Thor had circled the perimeter as he'd been trained to do. They were still in the clearing but pointed back the way they'd come. The Belgian snorted and turned his head to look at him, clearly questioning his lack of involvement in the program.

He took a cautious peek over his shoulder. Did Lani realize they'd stopped? She gave no indication of it. Head down, she appeared oblivious to her surroundings. Dear God, had she fallen asleep?

Then she quickly turned the page. Not asleep. Still reading.

He held his breath, mesmerized by the sight of Lani engrossed in his book. He couldn't ask for more than this.

She wasn't chuckling here, but she caught her breath a few times. An action scene? Or one where Dooley and Sophia try to resist the chemistry between them?

Leaning a little closer, he could almost see a section of the page, almost read the—

She suddenly looked up. With a startled cry she fell back against the seat.

He straightened. "Sorry. I was just—"

"I had no idea you were there!" She pressed a hand to her chest. "I'd just realized we'd stopped, and—"

"My apologies. I glanced around to see how you were doing."

"That was no *glance.* You were looming over me like... like you were ready to pounce or something."

He grimaced. Way to screw up the moment. "I was trying to see where you were."

Taking a quick breath, she focused on the manuscript on her lap. "I'm in the part where, um, she comes into the bar after closing to discuss the case and they're, um, having a... a moment."

"Ah." With her head down he could barely see the pink on her cheeks. His pulse ratcheted up a notch. She'd been affected. Probably didn't want to talk about it.

But he did. "The first kiss scene. What did you think?"

"It was good."

"Good enough?"

"Yes."

He sucked in air. "Thanks." Questions rose up, each one begging to be answered. How was the opening? What about the pacing? Could she visualize the setting?

He swallowed them all. "Ready for some hot chocolate?"

"Sure." Keeping her head down, she reached for the wrapping paper and tore off a small piece to use as a bookmark. She tucked it between the pages and returned the manuscript to the box.

"The snow's only a couple inches deep. Let's get down and stretch our legs." He hopped down.

"Works for me." Setting the box aside, she folded back the lap robe and stood.

He held out his hand, hoping she'd take it, not sure she would. She'd climbed in by herself. But she put her gloved hand in his. Two layers of glove didn't make for a very intimate connection, but she hadn't balked at letting him help her out.

When she had her footing, he let go and reached in to grab the backpack. She wandered a few feet away as he took out the ceramic mugs and thermos.

Pulling off his gloves, he shoved them in his pocket before unscrewing the lid on the thermos and pouring them each a cup. Steam rose from the surface, along with the sweet smell of sugar and chocolate.

He recapped the thermos and put it into the backpack. She stood several yards away, hands shoved in her pockets as she surveyed the meadow, clearly not wanting to focus on him.

He carried the mugs over. "Here you go."

She turned and accepted the mug he handed her. She'd ditched her gloves, too. "Smells delicious. Did you make it?"

"Granny did."

"That was nice of her."

"She's special."

"I think so, too." She lowered her lashes as she took a cautious sip. "Mm. Temperature's perfect."

"Drink up. It won't stay that way." He took a long swallow.

"Nothing ever does."

"Getting philosophical on me, Lani-lou?"

Awareness flashed in her hazel eyes, as it always did when he called her that. Then it was gone, replaced with a frown of disapproval. "See, this is why I don't spend much time with you. You insist on calling me—"

"Because deep down, you like it."

"No, I don't."

"Tell the truth and shame the devil."

She sighed. "I doubt it would work. You're completely shameless."

"You're calling me a devil?" Not really a bad thing, in his estimation. Put the word *sexy* in front of it and he'd take that compliment any day.

"You're a sly, sneaky devil. You've never once mentioned you had an interest in writing."

"Because I don't."

"The hell you don't. You've—"

"I don't have an *interest* in writing. It's the core of who I am, the only thing I've ever wanted to do."

"Then why doesn't anybody know about it?"

"Because I'm the son of a *New York Times* bestseller who's been a force in the industry for decades. By the time I was born she was already highly acclaimed. I could have instant access to agents and publishers. My work would be taken seriously from the minute it crossed somebody's desk."

"Most writers would kill for that opportunity."

"Not if they stopped to think about it. Oh, I could probably get published by a major house, probably even hers, but I'd never know if it was my writing or my mother's influence that got me there."

"I see." She sipped her hot chocolate and went back to admiring the scenery.

He was dying to ask her opinion of what she'd read, but he'd be damned if he'd do it. He'd wait her out. She'd have to tell him sometime. That was her job.

She tipped her head back to get the last drop from the mug. Then she dragged in a breath. "Judging from the chapters I've read, you don't need your mother's influence."

He stared at her, not quite processing what she'd said. "It's good?"

"It's crazy good. I suppose it could fall apart at any point, but—"

"Crazy good?" Joy bubbled in his chest, pushing him to do something wild and stupid to commemorate this moment.

"I didn't want to put it down. It's—"

"Sorry, Lani-lou, but I gotta kiss you." Tossing his mug in the snow, he nudged back his hat and pulled her close. Then he claimed her mouth before she had time to say no.

Maybe she'd bite him. Maybe she'd hit him upside the head with her empty mug. It was a risk he was willing to take.

4

What the hell? Rance had some kind of nerve, grabbing her like this! Lani opened her mouth to protest. Too late. He was there.

What now? She could clock him with the mug in her hand, but an unconscious Rance could be a problem. Probably best to stand there and do nothing. He'd hate that.

Unfortunately he'd caught her with her mouth open. He used that to his advantage, settling in, getting frisky with his tongue. He had technique. Should've guessed he'd be good at this.

Uh-oh. A quiver of desire started low in her belly and worked its way through her system. Heat spread everywhere, relaxing her rigid muscles, smoothing away her resistance.

His soft groan told her he could feel it. Cupping her tush, he tucked her in close and thrust his tongue deep.

Her body got the message and responded with embarrassing enthusiasm. Had she ground her hips against his? His low chuckle gave her the answer. She should've clocked him with the mug.

Time to put a stop to this nonsense. And she would. But since it was a one-time event never to be repeated, she could enjoy it a little bit long—

"We need to stop." His gentle murmur caressed her damp lips with a brush of air.

He was calling a halt? That was her job! She wiggled away from him, out of breath and pretending she wasn't. "What's this *we* business? I didn't agree to that kiss. That was all your idea."

"Yes, ma'am."

"And wipe that smug smile off your face. You caught me in a weak moment. I recently… broke up with someone."

"Oh? I'm sorry."

"You don't look sorry."

"Okay, I'm not. I'm the opposite of sorry. But I didn't know you were in a relationship. Did you mention him in August? Because I don't remember anything about—"

"I wasn't involved with him then."

"A short relationship."

"Almost four months!"

"A medium-sized relationship?"

"A significant one. Transformative."

"Uh-huh. Super smart guy. Lousy in the sack."

She fought the urge to laugh. "You could say that."

He tugged on the brim of his hat in a typical Rance gesture. "I believe I just did." A seductive glimmer lit his brown eyes. "Then you weren't reacting to me with that hip action. You're just extremely frustrated after spending four months with a dude who couldn't find a G-spot if his life depended on it."

Hit by a wave of lust, she nearly tackled him. "Yep." If he was willing to hand her a logical excuse for her behavior, she'd take it.

"In that case, I'm happy to offer my services."

"Rance!" Her face grew hot along with the rest of her. "Good grief! I'm not going to have an affair with you."

"Why not? You have an itch. I'm happy to scratch it. That's perfectly legit in the twenty-first century."

"It's a trap. You want me to fall in love with you and move to Rowdy Ranch."

"You're a level-headed woman. I'm sure you wouldn't confuse good sex with love."

"You're right, I wouldn't, but even if I considered it, which I won't, there's the matter of logistics. I'm in my folks' cabin and you have Granny living in yours." Why was she even discussing it with him? *Because you want to, dummy.*

"Facing the roadblocks is the first step toward removing them."

"We can't remove them. I'm not sneaking you into my parents' guest room and I can't imagine frolicking in yours with Granny right across the hall."

He grinned. "Frolicking is such a great word. I'll bet you didn't frolic with what's-his-name."

Not because she hadn't tried. "I'm not going to frolic with you, either." But how she wished she could.

"What if I told you I've discussed the possibility with Granny and she's all for it?"

"*What?*"

"I do believe you're more prudish than she is. Last week, before you and your folks arrived, she brought up the subject."

"On her own?"

"Absolutely. I swear she can read my mind. I was talking about the sleighride, and out of the blue she says, *Ya know, luv, I'm in bed by nine and out like a light.* Then she winked at me."

"But she's still in the cabin. Unless you've soundproofed your bedroom... oh, wait. I can picture you doing that."

His eyebrows arched. "Can you, now?" He looked more pleased than insulted.

"I wouldn't put anything past you."

"I'll take that as a compliment."

"It isn't."

He shrugged. "If you say so. Anyway, Granny had a follow-up. *I took to wearin' earplugs to block m'oul fella's snorin' and now they're a comfort even if it makes no sense anymore. Once I take out m'hearin' aids and put in m'earplugs, it's deaf as a post I am.*"

"Wow, you sound just like her. So does the granny in your story, by the way."

"Thanks. I've worked hard on her character. But we're straying from the topic of roadblocks. Which are now gone."

Desire curled within her, as it did whenever he looked at her with that knowing gleam in his eyes. He saw past her defenses and knew exactly how he tempted her. "It's still not a good idea."

"Are you sure about that?"

"Positive. Granny's a matchmaker. Her comments prove she's paving the way hoping we'll end up together. When that doesn't happen, she'll be bitterly disappointed. Do you want that on your conscience?"

"Good argument, wrong premise. She's determined to find me a wife, but if you don't work out she won't waste time being bitterly disappointed. She'll move on to the next candidate."

"Oh." One argument down, but she had more. "She's not the only person who'd like to see us become a couple. If there's even a hint that might happen, my folks would get their hopes up. It's why I almost didn't make this trip."

That clearly shocked him. "Because of me?"

"Because of the whole setup. While no one's pressuring me to move, they would love it if I did. Last night at dinner Mom and Dad suggested I could go remote and use their air miles whenever I need to fly back East."

"Would that be so bad?"

"Yes. Square Glasses Press is a small, intimate operation so I'm not just editing manuscripts. I'm in on all of it — cover designs, launch dates, marketing strategies. We brainstorm stuff and gather in the conference room on the spur-of-the-moment. I'd miss out on a lot."

"You love it there."

"I do."

He sighed. "I can't argue with that. I feel the same about the ranch. If writing ends up making me a lot of money and I could live anywhere, I still wouldn't leave."

"Which means you need to find a woman who loves it like you do."

"Excellent point."

"That's not me."

"Ah, but the place is growing on you."

"Sure it is. The setting's magnificent and the people are great."

"Including yours truly?"

She gazed at him. If only he didn't look so damn sexy standing there, his hat cocked at a rakish angle, a half-smile tilting his talented mouth. "No comment."

"You won't let yourself like me."

"Because you're a pain in the ass."

"That may be, but I guarantee I can find your G-spot."

"Stop it." Warmth cascaded through her, finding all her secret places.

"What if we agree we're not meant for each other and we'll just have sex because it'll feel good?"

"That's what Sara told herself when she met Kieran and you see how that turned out."

"You're not Sara. You're made of sterner stuff."

"I'm not having an affair with you, Rance."

"Tell you what. Don't decide yet."

"I've already decided and the answer is no." It had to be. If she stepped too close to the fire, she'd get burned.

"What if, after you finish the book, you come over for a Granny-cooked dinner so the three of us can discuss it and also plan how we're going to do the big reveal for the family."

"I might not finish for several days."

He shook his head. "You were hooked. You'll finish it by tomorrow if not sooner."

"Not necessarily." But he was right. Again. "Even if I finish it tomorrow, how can I justify going to your cabin for dinner?"

"Because we won't play it like that. You just say you want Granny to check the authenticity of an Irish character in a manuscript you're reading and all you have is the hard copy, which is the absolute truth."

"That works. In fact, I don't have to read your book in secret, do I? I can say it's a submission, which it is."

"Just don't let anybody see my name on it."

"I can manage that."

"So the manuscript gets you over to my place, and then you text your folks to say Granny invited you to dinner."

"What if they need the truck?"

"Don't take it. I work eleven to five tomorrow. I'll pick you up on my way home."

"It's not on your way home."

"I'll make a small detour. It's the gentlemanly thing to do. The point is, we'll have dinner, she'll go to bed and we can decide if we want to go to bed, too."

Her heart started playing the bongos. "That's crazy."

"Might be crazy good."

She didn't doubt it. Did she dare indulge herself for a couple of hours? "I can't stay the night."

"I'm not asking you to. I'll take you back long before your parents wake up. No one has to know except Granny, and even she won't know for sure."

"You could only pull that trick once."

"I know."

"So that'll be it. One and done."

"That depends on whether I've sufficiently scratched your itch. If I have, we'll call it quits. If I haven't, I'll dream up another scenario. Are you in?"

Anticipation made her shaky. "I'll think about it."

"You're in."

"I didn't say that!"

His smile widened. "No, but your eyes did."

5

Rance wanted to kiss Lani again, but he'd discovered that kissing made him desperate for something he couldn't have right now. "We should head back." He picked up the mug lying in the snow. "I'll take yours."

"Tell Granny I loved her hot chocolate."

"I will." He walked toward the sleigh and she fell into step beside him. "There's more if you want some before we leave."

"I'd rather just go. I want to get back to your book."

"Excellent news." Shoving the mugs into the backpack, he zipped it. "I guess that means you don't want to drive, either."

"No, thanks."

"Then up you go." He held out a hand and she took it to steady herself. This time it was skin on skin and he tightened his grip, relishing the contact, imagining her touch on other places, sexy places.

Maybe he shouldn't count his chickens, but he'd laid out a fool-proof plan. She hadn't been able to poke holes in it and her days of pretending she didn't want him were over.

He'd taken a huge chance acting on impulse, though. He'd originally talked himself out of kissing her while they were in the meadow, but apparently it hadn't been too soon after all.

The manuscript hadn't hurt his cause, either. Writing a book to woo a bookworm made sense assuming the content didn't suck.

Evidently it didn't, judging from the way she settled into her seat and immediately opened the box. She was totally immersed in the story before he'd made it up to the driver's box. Slapping the lines against Thor's rump, he told the Belgian to get moving and off they went.

Crazy good. He'd instantly deposited those two words in his memory bank. As Thor trotted down the path, the bells on his harness jingled and the sleigh runners whispered over a perfect carpet of pure white snow. The Christmas spirit was alive and well today.

Unless Lani found major problems in the rest of the book, Square Glasses Press would take it. He'd researched the company and read the reviews of their recent publications. Decent reviews, but no blockbusters. Fine with him. He hadn't given the book to Lani expecting her publisher to make him a bestseller.

She was right that he'd have had a better chance using his mother's contacts. But going that route wasn't his style.

The ride back went faster, or at least it seemed that way. When they made a right onto his mom's road, he glanced over his shoulder. "We're almost there. I'm gonna stop so you can put that away and climb up here."

"Can we just sit here for a few minutes? I want to finish this scene."

Thor snorted and shook his head, setting off the bells. Then he turned his head and gazed back at them.

Lani peered at the Belgian. "I'll bet you want to go home."

"He does."

"Okay. Never mind. I'll stop."

Her eagerness to keep reading scattered an extra handful of glitter on an already sparkling day. He hopped down and waited for her to box up the manuscript. "When you get to the end, would you please call me?"

"Not if it's the middle of the night." She tucked the wrapping paper in with it and closed the lid.

"Definitely call me if it's the middle of the night. That means you stayed up late to finish it and I'll want to hear why you did."

"It might be two in the morning." She laid the lap robe over the box and put the bow in her pocket. "I've been known to forget the time."

"I don't care. Call me. I know you have my number since I put it in your phone the last time you were here."

"And maybe I deleted it."

"Did you?" That would be discouraging.

"No."

He smiled.

"I've been busy."

"Call me. Please."

"All right, if you insist." She took his hand as she stepped down.

"I sure want to kiss you right now."

She glanced up. "Well, don't."

"I'm not gonna, but I'll be thinking about our first kiss a lot."

"Not me."

"Liar."

She held his gaze. "Yeah, I'll think about it, too. Come on." She tugged him toward the front of the sleigh. "I want to drive."

"Yes, ma'am." He helped her up, climbed in beside her and handed her the lines. "Just slap these lightly on his rump and tell him to go."

"Move out, Thor!" The Belgian took off without her having to tap him with the lines, which made her laugh. "He really does want to go home."

"He knows I brought him some carrot chunks."

"Where are they?"

"In my truck. You don't have to stick around for that, since you probably want to get back to reading. Just take the box and vamoose."

"That's not fair. I'll help you unhitch and brush him."

"Nah, I've got this." They rounded the bend in the road. "And I'll have help. See Buck walking up to the barn? He must have figured we'd be back about now."

"Should I try to hide the box under my coat? I'm not sure I can. It'll look like I'm smuggling something."

"It doesn't matter if he sees it. He knows I gave you a Christmas present, just not what it was."

"Then he knows you're interested in me?"

"He does. Quite a few people know. They just think you don't like me."

"I'm not sure I do."

"Fair enough."

"What if he asks me about the gift?"

"Just tell him it's a book you've always wanted."

"We've established I'm not a convincing liar."

"And here I thought you've been hoping I'd write a book so you could read it. I'm crushed."

"You don't crush easily. Okay, I'll tell him— I don't know what I'll tell him. I'll think of something."

"Now you're starting to sound like me, creating subterfuge on the fly." He waved at Buck, who waved back.

"But the difference is you love intrigue. You eat it up with a spoon while it makes me nervous as hell."

"Because you don't do it enough. You've got the brains for it, just not the nerve. Stick with me and you'll get better."

"That's what I'm afraid of."

"Don't worry, Lani-lou. I've got your back."

She groaned. "What would it take to get you to stop calling me that?"

"I'd tell you, but you can't afford it."

"You want me to *pay you*? That's extreme, even for you."

"I'm not talking about money."

"Oh, I see. Since I'm bargaining with the devil, I guess you want my soul."

"No, but you're close."

Her breath hitched. "You're right. I can't afford it." As they drew closer to the barn, she surveyed the area in front of it. "Where do you want me to park this rig?"

"Anywhere. We'll haul it back to the tractor barn after we take care of Thor. You can stop here, if you want."

"Okay, then. Whoa, Thor! Whoa, boy!"

When the sleigh came to a halt, Rance leaped down. He started to help Lani but paused to glance up at her. Buck was on his way over. "Want to climb down by yourself?"

"Yes, I do."

"I'll get the box."

"Hey, guys," Buck called out. "I see you're back in one piece. Hang on, Lani, I'll help you down."

"Thanks."

Rance ducked his head to hide a smile. Buck would chastise him later for his lapse in cowboy manners. Retrieving the box, he turned and waited while Buck played the gentleman.

Then he handed Lani the box. "I know it wasn't exactly what you expected, but—"

"It's great." She kept her expression neutral. "Thank you for thinking of me. And for the sleigh ride. I'll just stick this in the truck so I can help with Thor."

"Speaking of the truck, you probably need to take it back in case your folks want to go somewhere."

"Oh. I suppose—"

"Don't worry about Thor," Buck said. "Rance and I can handle this. We don't want to strand Harry and Vanessa."

"No, we don't. I wish now I'd rented a car, but they insisted I didn't need to."

Buck nodded. "They wanted to save you money. By all means, go."

"I'll see you two later, then. Thanks again for the sleigh ride. It was fun." She hurried away.

"She hated your gift, didn't she?"

Rance turned to Buck, who for years had been the only father figure in his life. He couldn't tell Buck the surface details, but he could give him the truth underneath those facts. "She actually really liked it."

"You're kidding yourself, son. She said it was great, but she didn't mean it. Anyone could tell that. Oh, and her saying *thank you for thinking of me*? That's what everyone says when your gift bombs."

"Take my word for it, the gift didn't bomb."

"Then why did she react that way?"

"Because she's afraid to like anything connected to me. Deep down, she believes I have the power to ruin her life."

"Do you?"

"Maybe." That worried him more than he cared to admit.

6

Lani arrived at her parents' cabin as they were fixing an early lunch prior to heading into town. After some last-minute Christmas shopping they'd have dinner at the Buffalo.

When they invited her to go along, she told them the truth. She had to finish reading a manuscript by tomorrow.

It wasn't a lie, but it felt like one. She'd left a lot unsaid and she wasn't used to keeping secrets from her folks. But Rance's book wasn't her secret. It was his, and he'd entrusted it to her. Her feelings about that ran the gamut.

If the book had been carelessly written, something he'd tossed off as an excuse to reel her in, she would have been furious. But there was nothing careless about this effort. Even seasoned professionals had typos. She'd found only one so far.

To be fair, she might have missed a few. Sophia and Dooley kept her so enthralled that she'd settled for a peanut butter sandwich and called it dinner so she could keep reading.

Rance had successfully mirrored the sassy tone of *Moonlighting* and taken it up a notch. Those two were hysterical together.

And hot. After their first kiss, she'd wondered how far Rance would go with the relationship. She'd put on her pajamas and climbed into bed by the time she found out. He'd written the most sensual love scene she'd ever read. Flushed and aroused, she closed her eyes and relived the moment Rance's mouth had claimed hers.

If he made love the way he'd written this scene....

The sound of her parents' truck pulling in blasted through her lusty thoughts. Scrambling out of bed, she closed her door and switched off the light.

The front door opened and they came in, laughing about something. "Lani?" her mother called. "We're back. I wish you'd—"

Then her dad murmured something.

"I guess you're right," her mom said. "There's no light under her door. The sleigh ride must have tuckered her out." Her retreating footsteps, muted conversation and more laughter indicated they might stay up for a while longer.

She wouldn't have to continue playing possum, though. They'd designed their cabin with two generously sized bedrooms on either side of the house with the living room and kitchen in the middle. She had plenty of privacy and her own bathroom.

That didn't mean she was willing to smuggle Rance in here, even if that sounded extremely appealing at the moment. She sat in the dark, her palms flat against the manuscript as if she could somehow make physical contact with him through the printed words.

Had she reacted to the scene more fully because she'd kissed the author? Maybe, but she couldn't deny he'd done a magnificent job.

The beautifully written sensual encounter was a potent spice flavoring a juicy meal of action, suspense and humor. She rarely found that combo in a first timer, especially if the writer was male.

The editor in her was dazzled. The woman had been thoroughly seduced. Was he counting on that? She'd always known he was clever. And devious. And full of the devil.

She hadn't credited him with patience. He'd planned this for almost a year. He'd cultivated his friendship with Sara, who'd become his ally.

Meanwhile he'd worked in secret with the goal of handing over a finished manuscript to a woman who loved words and delighted in those who used them well. He'd made himself damn near irresistible.

Admiration warred with alarm. She'd seriously underestimated Rance McLintock. She was dealing with a mastermind.

Switching on the light, she returned her attention to Sophia and Dooley — or more accurately, Lani and Rance. She saw him as Dooley, now. Every female reader would once they got a look at a publicity shot of Rance in a Stetson, his cocky smile fueling their fantasies.

Authors always claimed they weren't their characters, and some things about Dooley didn't fit Rance. For one thing, he didn't keep a gun behind the bar. He'd never, at least to her knowledge, been a deputy.

But he had an Irish granny who sounded just like the woman temporarily living in his cabin. And he was crazy about Sophia, a brunette with hazel eyes.

This was a series, so the tug-of-war between the characters wouldn't be resolved in this story or the ones that followed. She doubted Rance envisioned that scenario for his personal story, though.

He wanted a resolution and he was pulling out all the stops to get it. Unfortunately for him, he'd picked the wrong woman. Eventually he'd figure that out.

Meanwhile, she had a book submission to finish. She let herself sink back into Dooley and Sophia's world.

She took her time. The prose was delicious, chock-full of words and phrases that deserved to be savored. As with all her favorite books, she hated to see it end.

When it did, she wanted the next one in the series. Immediately. Had he even started it? One way to find out. She picked up her phone.

He answered on the first ring. "You're done?"

"Just now." She glanced at the time on her screen. "Good Lord, it's two-thirty."

"Never mind that. Tell me what you think."

"My boss would hate me for saying this, but you need a bigger house, one that can get you on the *Times* list. You deserve to be there."

"Thank you." His voice sounded husky.

"Are you okay? Did I wake you?"

"No, ma'am."

"I'll bet I did. Your voice is a little froggy."

"I'm just... very happy." He cleared his throat. "Very happy indeed."

He wasn't sleepy. He'd sounded gruff because he was touched by what she'd said. That was sweet. And sexy. "I'm serious. You should take this to a major house."

"I'd need an agent unless I want it buried in the slush pile for years."

"Ask your mom's agent to pitch it without mentioning you're her son."

"So a publisher buys it without knowing who I am, but they'll find out soon enough. Besides, I don't want to be a cog in a big machine. Even Mom doesn't always get what she wants. I figure a small press gives me a better chance of having a say in the process."

"You would. We pride ourselves on listening to the author's ideas and implementing them whenever possible."

"And you know me personally. I'm not just some guy off the street. But like I said on the sleighride, the main reason I gave it to you is—"

"You wanted me to read the sexy scenes."

"No! I mean, yeah, I did, but—"

"I knew it! The book is part of your master plan to—"

"I wanted an unbiased opinion."

"Of the sex scenes?'

"Of the whole thing!"

"There's no bias regarding the rest of it, but I can't say that about the sex scenes."

"Why not?"

"Because you *kissed me,* genius! You think that didn't change how I read the sensual parts? That it didn't make them twice as hot?"

He chuckled. "So they worked for you."

"Of course, but I can't pretend that my opinion of those scenes lacks bias. Not after you laid one on me."

"Good to know." Laughter rippled through his words. "Maybe I should limber up my lips before a signing and kiss every woman who buys the book. Interesting marketing strategy."

Talking about his lips was not a good idea. She needed to hang up and calm down. "Anyway, you have my evaluation. Have a good night, what's left of it."

"Lani, wait."

His low, urgent tone sent a surge of heat through her overstimulated body. "What?"

"What you said about my book, the confidence you have in it — that's huge. I can't let you hang up without letting you know how much it means. You've given me the best Christmas gift of my life. If you hadn't liked it, I... well, I don't know what I would have done."

"It's only one person's opinion, Rance."

"But yours is the one I trust. You may be the only one I fully trust to tell me the unvarnished truth."

"You're giving me too much power."

"That's where you're wrong. You can't imagine how much power you wield when it comes to me."

The vulnerability in that statement stole her breath. "I don't know what to say to that."

"Just say you'll come over tomorrow night."

"Listen, we really shouldn't—"

"I know. I get it. Come over for Granny. Let her feed you. She'll want to hear everything you have to say about the book. She's been almost as anxious about what you'd think of it as I have. Just have dinner. You don't have to stay."

"You won't try to talk me into it?"

"No, ma'am."

"All right then."

"Great. I'll pick you up about five-thirty. Bring the book."

"Of course. Good night, Rance."

"Good night, Lani. Sweet dreams."

She disconnected. Sweet dreams, indeed. She'd have dreams, but guaranteed they wouldn't be sweet.

Dinner with Granny while they talked about the future of Rance's excellent book would be tons of fun. He wouldn't coax her to stay. He was too smart for that. And more patient than she ever would have believed.

He'd give her the choice. She just had to make the right one.

7

Rance always looked forward to working at the Buffalo the week before Christmas. Customers ordered fancy holiday drinks, the band played seasonal favorites, the wooden buffalo had a different greeting every day and his boss Tyra went all out with decorations.

But tonight he couldn't wait to get the hell out of there when his shift ended at five. Snow was predicted, but it hadn't started yet as he headed out of town. The deserted two-lane highway illuminated by Thunder's high beams was clear and dry.

He nudged the needle a tad over the speed limit, enough to shorten the trip some but not enough to get pulled over. He couldn't wait to see Lani, but he'd lowered his expectations about how tonight would go.

He wanted her in his life. He'd convinced himself he could make that happen if he took his time, and when her entire family moved to Rowdy Ranch, he'd thought he had it in the bag.

He'd overheard her folks tell his mom they hoped the air miles offer would convince her to switch to working remotely. He'd assumed she'd agree. That had left him only one task — turning her lust for him into love. He'd been prepared to give it all he had.

He'd counted on the book to play a big part in the effort. He hadn't intended to fall for an editor, but clearly Fate had a sense of humor.

Granny was his other ace in the hole and she'd offered to coach him on how to conduct a serious relationship. She'd only known Lani from pictures and family stories. Didn't matter. If Rance wanted her, Granny was geared up to help make it happen.

But after the way Lani had described her work setup, he'd faced reality. Remote work wouldn't cut it, which put a serious crimp in his plan. He wasn't giving up, but he didn't have answers, either. This morning he'd told Granny he was backing off a little and she'd approved of that decision.

The new digs for the senior Armstrongs featured an old-fashioned lamp post beside the turnoff to their cabin. They'd asked Angie and her crew to install one similar to those lining Main Street.

Now everyone wanted one, especially after they saw how it looked decorated with a wreath and a big red bow. Between family jobs and out-of-town gigs, business was booming for Angie's small company.

She gave partial credit to the new name — *Two Handywomen and an Irishman*. Kieran's impressive skills added to its reputation, but some folks scheduled a project just to hear him talk.

Harry and Vanessa's yellow truck was gone, so good thing Lani hadn't planned on driving herself over. He'd washed Thunder this morning in honor of her first ride in his rig. He'd had to remove and reinstall the reindeer antlers and the wreath on the front grill, but the occasion warranted the effort.

Thunder glittered in the glow of Christmas lights strung across the front porch. A decorated tree stood in the front window and a large pine wreath hung on the door. Before he could shut off the engine, Lani came out, coat and hat on and a tote bag over her shoulder.

His heart stuttered as it did whenever he caught sight of her. She'd been a challenge to his equilibrium from the get-go, unlike Sara, who'd felt like a long-lost buddy.

His reaction to Lani had confused him until Lucky said he might be falling in love for the first time in his life. Lucky had called it.

Leaving the motor running, he hopped out. "I see your folks took off."

"They're having dinner with Andy and your mom. They suggested we all come over after Granny's checked the manuscript."

"She's already started cooking." He helped her into Thunder's passenger seat.

"Then I'll let them know." She reached into the tote for her phone.

"You and I could drop by later, if you want to tell them that."

Her gaze met his, held for a moment. Then she took a quick breath. "Let's not complicate things."

"Okay." He closed the door and hurried around to the driver's side. He would give anything to know what had gone through her mind just now. But he wouldn't ask.

When he climbed behind the wheel and shut the door, he let out a sigh of pleasure. Thunder's cab had never felt so cozy. Was it wrong to wish the drive to his cabin would take longer?

"Tough day?"

"No. Why'd you ask?" He shifted into reverse and backed the truck around so he could pull out.

"That big sigh of relief."

"I've looked forward to seeing you. And now you're here. We're on our way. That was a contented sigh you just heard."

"Oh." A pause. "I've looked forward to seeing you, too."

He glanced over. She stared out the windshield, not looking at him, but the light from the dash allowed him to see the flush on her cheek. "Does that mean you're starting to like me a little bit?"

"I like Dooley a lot."

"I'm glad, but he's not me. I've never been in law enforcement and never had a desire to be. If that's what you admire about him, then—"

"It isn't. He's a reluctant hero. That's always appealed to me."

"Well, I'm about as reluctant a hero as you'll ever find."

"That's what I mean. You sounded like Dooley just then. And he sounds like you."

"I suppose that's inevitable."

"Does he think like you?"

"About what?" Her line of questioning made him nervous.

"Women."

He swallowed. He knew a trap when he saw one. "Could you be more specific?"

"Sure. Does he think about Sophia the way you think about me?"

He couldn't tell from her tone whether that would be a plus or a minus. What would Granny do? She'd tell the truth. "Yes, he does. Full disclosure, I thought about you when I created Sophia and if that bothers you, I can change—"

"Don't change anything. It's... it's lovely."

"Yeah?" Which was nice to hear, but something was wrong. The air crackled with tension.

"You're a shapeshifter, Rance." Her voice quivered. "I took you for a jokester, a man skating on the surface of life, and then I read this book and discover you have depth and empathy and sensitivity, or at least Dooley does. And now I don't... I don't know what to..."

Her audible gulp told him she was losing it. He pulled over and shifted into park. "I'm sorry." He unbuckled his seat belt and turned to her. "You're right. You saw me one way and I played to that while working on a plan to dramatically change your opinion."

Taking a shaky breath, she shoved her hands in the pockets of her coat. "Which you did, damn you." She flashed him a look hot enough to set his clothes on fire. "I can't get those scenes out of my head."

He didn't have to ask which scenes she meant. "I was operating on a false premise. So many people work remote these days and I thought—"

"I know what you thought. So did my parents. And Sara. Everybody assumed by the first of the year I'd be living here. But I won't. And now... now there's *you*." She flung it as an accusation.

And he stood accused.

8

"Is there anything I can do to fix this?" Rance looked destroyed, poor guy.

Well, he should feel guilty. He'd created a mess. "I doubt it." Although Lani appreciated his sincere offer and his willingness to take the blame, he couldn't do anything to douse the fire licking through her veins. Or could he? "Maybe there is something."

"Name it."

"Chewing tobacco."

He grimaced.

"That would desexify you in no time."

"That's not a word."

"It is now. Keep a chaw stuck under your lip and carry around a can so you can spit tobacco juice from time to time. Instant desexification."

"Also not a word." He hesitated. "How about bubblegum? If I'm popping bubbles all the time, wouldn't that be desexifying?"

"Nah, I'd just laugh. Besides, I like the taste of bubblegum."

"Jalapeno peppers?"

"Yum."

"Chewing tobacco it is, then. I'll buy some tomorrow."

"You'd do it?"

"To desexify myself so you're not in distress? Yes, ma'am, I would cheerfully take up that disgusting habit."

"And there it is."

"There what is?"

"The way you're reacting is just like Dooley. You're accepting responsibility and you want to help. On top of it you're sexy as hell. How am I supposed to resist you?"

"That was the idea. I didn't want you to. But now I need to reverse the process, so if keeping a chaw under my lip does the trick, then I'll—"

"Guess what? It won't. Not when I know you're suffering for my sake. Besides, Granny would have a fit. So would the rest of your family. It's a terrible idea. I just wish I could block out those sexy scenes in your book."

"Hey, that's the answer."

"You have a technique to erase a memory? That's disturbing."

"Not erase. Reframe. You don't want me, you want Dooley, and he doesn't exist. Compared to him, I'm lousy in the sack. You'd be in for a big letdown."

"I don't believe you." Neither did the parts of her that began to tingle.

"Come on. It's way easier to write good sex than to deliver in person. Logic will tell you that."

The warmth gathering in her core had kicked logic to the curb. "More likely I'd be a disappointment to you. Sophia's so responsive and I—"

His eyes glittered. "You just spent four months with a dud. Whatever went on with him doesn't count."

A surge of lust took her breath away. "You're not helping."

"You were about to put yourself down. I've kissed you, and there's nothing unresponsive about—"

"Listen, insisting you won't measure up to Dooley isn't helping." It made her desperate to find out. Heat radiated to every part of her body.

"But he's a figment of my imagination."

She gulped for air. "Exactly! Which indicates you'd be imaginative in—"

"Not when all the blood flows south!"

"You turn into a mindless sex machine?" That worked, too. She wanted that. She wanted it *now.*

"Sometimes, damn it!" His chest heaved. "I mean, not always, but—"

"We should change the subject."

"Right." He faced forward and gripped the steering wheel with both hands.

"It's pointless to sit here talking about whether we'll have good sex or bad sex."

"I didn't say it would be bad."

"Granny must wonder what's keeping us."

He dragged in a breath. "She will." Buckling up, he put the truck in gear.

Silence. But not complete silence. His unsteady breathing told her that he was thinking about exactly what she was thinking about.

She cleared her throat. "What are we having for dinner?"

"Shepherd's pie. You'll love it."

"If it's the one with mashed potatoes on top, I know I will."

"It is."

"Is Granny spoiling you?"

"Me and everyone she can get her hands on." His breathing began to even out. "My kitchen has never been this busy."

"Did you add Dooley's granny before or after she arrived here?"

"A little of both. Dooley already had a grandmother, but once I saw a picture of Kieran's granny, I gave the one in my book a makeover."

"I'll bet she changed even more after Granny moved in."

"You have no idea. I had to be careful or she would've taken over the story."

Tension still rippled between them, but it was manageable. "Have you started the next one?"

"Last night."

"That's what you were doing when I called?"

"It was the only thing that kept me from going crazy waiting to hear from you."

That was sobering. "I guess we're both walking an emotional tightrope."

"I'll never admit to that."

"You just did." She glanced over at him.

His cheek dented. "No, ma'am, I did not. You'll never catch me on a tightrope. Those dudes wear spangled tights."

"They're ripped dudes in spangled tights."

"But the outfit's the problem. Cowboys don't do spangled tights."

"How about saying you've got barbed wire tangled around your Wranglers?"

He chuckled. "I could say that."

And he could melt her heart in the process. "You really expected this to work out, didn't you?"

He sighed. "Yep."

"Looking at it from your vantage point, I can see why. All the signs pointed to me deciding to move out here. But I'm still blown away that you hatched this plan in February. Did you really set your sights on me months ago?"

"Uh-huh."

His answer sent squiggles through her stomach. "But you flirted with both me and Sara."

"I did at first. Then you two sat me down and said I had to choose. For the first time in my life I paid close attention to my gut as well as my cock. I can trust my gut a lot more."

"Mm." And they were back on dangerous ground. Not his fault. She'd asked.

"You're both beautiful, both sexy, but you... you stir something deeper in me. You inspired me to get off my butt and begin writing this series."

"If I did, I'm glad. But I'm pretty sure I haven't flirted back."

"You have not. I'd given you no reason to, but that's because I'd never let you see who I am."

Her chest tightened. "Seems like you've kept that from everyone."

"Not quite true. Lucky knows me. He's not going to be shocked that I've been writing. Mom won't be, either. It's possible nobody in my family will be completely surprised. I think they know I've been up to something and it's somehow connected to you."

"What do you mean?"

"I'm sure they've noticed I haven't dated since February, which isn't like me. They probably assume it's because I've made a choice."

He hadn't been seeing other women? She didn't want to hear that. "I can see why you didn't date. This book must have taken all your free time."

"Not all of it. I still went dancing at the Buffalo now and then. I've been known to take a woman home after a night of dancing but I quit doing that in February. Getting horizontal with anyone other than you didn't appeal to me."

He'd saved himself for her. "How can you be so committed to someone you barely know?"

"I'm a writer. We soak up info like a sponge. I made good use of that week you and your family stayed here after Angie got married. When your folks came in May, I learned more about you. August was the best, though, when we took that ride."

"But we had a fight!"

"Do you remember what it was about?"

"Yes! It was about... oh, my God. It was about whether a man is capable of writing sex as well as a woman can."

"Great discussion. If you enjoyed the scenes I wrote, you can thank yourself. I should probably mention you in the acknowledgments."

"Don't you dare."

"I'm kidding. I wouldn't do that. Our fight was private and special. That's when I knew for sure you're the one."

"Oh, Rance, no I'm not."

"I'm afraid you are. That doesn't mean it'll work out. I've faced the fact it's up in the air for now. But my gut and my cock agree. I know you don't want to hear it, Lani-lou, but you're the one."

9

To Rance's surprise, Lani hadn't dinged him for calling her Lani-lou. Or told him he was delusional. Or an idiot. He'd apparently stunned her into silence with that last speech.

If she had more to say, she'd have to make it quick. They'd arrived. As he pulled in, Granny came out on the porch, her green checked apron over her dress, but no coat or hat.

"Doggone it." He threw the gearshift into park and hopped out. "Sorry we're a little late! Please go back in. It's freezing out here."

"Then ya didn't have a wreck or somethin'?"

"No. We're fine." He slammed the door and started around to the passenger side but Lani was already out.

"It's my fault, Granny." She hurried right past him. "I'm so sorry. I'm the one who made us late." She dashed up the steps. "I hope we didn't ruin your shepherd's pie."

"Just turned off the oven, I did. Texted ya, Rance, but ya didn't—"

"Must not have heard it." He took the steps two at a time and followed Lani though the door. He hung his hat on the coat rack. "Lani and I got to talking. It's nobody's fault. We lost track of—"

"Never ya mind, luv. Ya made it in one piece. Nothin' else matters, now, does it?" She turned to smile at them. "Take off yer coats, but stay outta the kitchen, both of ya. Turn yer backs ta the door. Don't be lookin' 'round. I've got ta set the scene."

"Set the scene?" Lani stopped so quickly that he nearly ran into her.

"My mum use ta set the scene when company came." She made a shooing motion with both hands. "Go on with ya. Look the other way."

Lani faced him with a cute little smile. "She means you, too, buster."

"Right." He turned and took a step back so he was standing beside her and could help her off with her coat.

Lani lowered her voice. "Do you know what she's up to?"

"I have no idea." He hung up her coat and his jacket.

"But you said you've had a lot of people over since she's been here. She didn't set the scene for them?"

"I guess there's company and then there's *company.*"

"Apparently."

"Just so you know, I told her working remotely is out. She understands the program is in jeopardy."

"It's always been in jeopardy. You just didn't realize it."

"But I do, now."

She glanced at him. "Do you?"

"Yes, ma'am." He held her gaze. "But that doesn't change—"

"Ya can come in!"

He gestured toward the arched kitchen doorway. "After you." He followed her into his kitchen, which now looked more like an exclusive bistro.

Granny had doused the overhead and pulled back the café curtains on the kitchen window. The multicolored glow of the Christmas lights on the porch railing blended with a slew of candles inside. Might be the entire batch he'd bought her a couple weeks ago.

A group of three sat on the table and others were spaced along the counters. He'd never seen that lace tablecloth before, or the lace-trimmed napkins tucked into gleaming silver napkin rings.

The matching silverware wasn't his, or the crystal wine glasses. "Where'd all this come from?"

"Had it in my wee hope chest, I did. There's a fourth napkin and place settin' if we ever need it."

Lani gazed at the setup. "It's absolutely beautiful, Granny. And champagne! What a treat."

Rance took another look. Sure enough, on the far side of the table, slightly hidden in the shadows, was the ice bucket he rarely used. In it sat the bottle of extremely pricey champagne his mom had given Granny when she'd first arrived.

"It's a celebration we'll be havin', isn't it? The book's done and ya gave it yer stamp of approval." Granny beamed at her. "Have a seat. "

"Which one?"

"The middle. Ya can see the lights on the porch from there. And the tree."

"I noticed the pretty lights when we drove in. But if there's a decorated tree out there, I didn't see it."

Granny chuckled. "Yer mind was on other things, luv. Look there." She pointed to a thirty-foot pine the entire family had decorated as a gift for Granny's first Christmas.

Ducking her head, Lani scanned the area. "Oh, my goodness! How did I miss that?" She glanced at him over her shoulder. "Did you rent a crane?"

"Angie did, and we all pitched in to get 'er done."

"Got a ride in the bucket, I did." Granny laughed. "Thirty feet in the air. Put the star on. ''Twas pure craic."

"It looks like the tree on the White House lawn. Who came up with the idea?"

"Lucky suggested it. Otherwise we'd have to take down my pool table so we could have a tree in the living room."

"I wouldn'ta let him dismantle that table to put up a tree. Anyway, there's a wee one in m'bedroom. Very festive. One in his, too."

He gave her a look. She gazed right back, her cherub face filled with innocence. He had to glance away or he'd start laughing. Granny was more of a schemer than he'd counted on. Champagne, indeed.

And it was delicious, a perfect complement to shepherd's pie, hot rolls and even Granny's Irish pound cake. They toasted the completion of his book and spent most of the meal talking about it.

He and Lani were careful not to give spoilers, though. He'd printed a second copy for Granny before leaving for work this morning, but she'd been too busy cooking to get very far.

Lani's copy lay on the table between her place and Granny's. Several times she'd flipped through it to quote a line she especially liked.

He soaked up every word of praise, every smile, every laugh of delight. She loved his book. Selfish man that he was, he craved more than that. He wanted her to love him.

And not just a little bit. He wanted her to love him so desperately she'd put her considerable intelligence to work finding a solution. If they both worked on the problem, they'd find a way. Necessity was the mother of invention, right?

"Will ya be tellin' your family, now?" Granny polished off her champagne. The bottle was nearly gone.

He'd had very little, but he'd kept the other two goblets filled. "I want to, but I haven't decided the best way to do it."

"Well, I have, lad. The two of ya could tell yer mum first, together, then tell the rest at a gatherin'."

He nodded. "Christmas Day, maybe."

"That's what I'm thinkin'. Ya don't hafta say I've known for months, either. No reason to. Say I just found out."

"But you've been so much help to me. You deserve some credit."

She waved a hand. "'Twas an honor. I'll be... what is it called? Oh, yeah. A silent partner."

"But—"

"It's how I want it. There's a chance yer mum would be hurt because I knew long before she did. I'd cut out m'heart before I'd cause her pain."

"Okay, then." He glanced at Lani. "Tomorrow's Sunday. Mom doesn't usually plan much for Sunday mornings, especially with Christmas only four days away."

"There's another reason to go tomorrow morning. Sara and Kieran will be at Lucky's. He and Oksana invited them to hang out for the day and help decorate their tree."

"Good. I keep forgetting they're still at the house. That makes it the perfect time to break the news. I could text her around eight and plan to go over around nine."

"What about Andy? Won't he be there?"

"Yes, and that's even more reason to do it tomorrow. She tells him everything so he might as well hear it when she does. I can pick you up."

"I need a plausible reason to be going over with you."

He shrugged. "Just say it's a surprise for Christmas. Everybody has secrets this time of year."

"True."

"You'll be needin' two copies, then — one for yer mum and one for Andy. Take mine."

"No need. I'll print another one between now and then."

"If you say so, but I'll be leavin' mine by the front door in case you run out of time."

"All right." He'd only have a time crunch if Lani stayed late. Judging from her pink cheeks, she'd come to the same conclusion. He picked up the champagne bottle. "There's still more. Who wants it?"

Granny waved him away. "Thank you kindly, but I've had plenty."

"Lani? We don't want it to go to waste."

"I'll split it with you."

"Done." He divided up what was left. His was gone in two swallows.

Lani took longer with hers. "That was a fabulous meal, Granny. Your pound cake is to die for."

"Take some home to yer folks, luv. Made it for 'em once before. Raved about it, they did."

"Thank you. I will."

"Good." She gazed at Lani. "Are ya sure ya can't do yer job usin that video thing Kieran tried to get me ta do? So what if it makes ya look bad?"

"That's not the problem."

"No? Rance said ya needed to be there so I thought ya didna like seein' yerself on the screen."

"Nope. Being on site is the whole point these days, ever since a new owner took over. Sasha reenergized the staff and now we all look forward to going in. One of my colleagues went remote and came back after two weeks. He said it was like taking a shower with his clothes on."

"'Tis a special job ya have, luv."

"It is."

Letting out a sigh, she pushed back her chair. "'Twas grand craic, but it's knackered I am. I hate ta leave ya both with the dishes, but—"

"I'll handle clean up." Rance stood and helped her out of her chair.

Lani got to her feet, too. "I'll help him. It's the least we can do after you fed us so well."

"I'll be toddlin' off, then." She gave Lani a hug and turned toward Rance.

He smiled. "I'll walk you to your room."

"Ah, yer a sweet one, boyo. I accept that gentlemanly gesture."

Lani started gathering the dishes. "I'll get things going in here."

"Thanks. I'll be right back." Rance followed Granny though the arched door and slipped an arm around her shoulders as they walked through the living room. "That was a wonderful meal and a beautiful setting. Thank you."

"Just tryin' to help."

"By adding a bottle of champagne?"

"Blame Ogden Nash."

"Who?"

"One of yer poets, he is. A Yank I dated before I met Kieran's grandpa was forever quotin' that fella. I've forgotten most of it, but one popped in ta m'head today. *Candy's dandy but liquor's quicker.*"

He cracked up. "Ah, Granny. What am I gonna do with you?"

"Never mind me. That woman's in love with ya. Do somethin' about it."

"But she—"

"Take my word for it, lad. Ya regret the things ya didna do more than the things ya did." Grasping his arm, she stood on her toes and kissed his cheek. "See ya in the mornin'." Without waiting for a response, she went into her room and shut the door.

He glanced toward the kitchen. Granny's parting advice butted up against the decision he'd made five minutes ago, to take Lani home after they cleaned up the kitchen.

That woman's in love with ya. Do somethin' about it.

Living past eighty didn't automatically make people wise. But Granny's counsel had served him well so far.

Lani had a say in it, though. If her answer was no, they'd skip the dishes, grab their coats and light out. If her answer was yes... they'd still skip the dishes.

_10_

Champagne had something to do with the fizzy sensation coursing through Lani's veins, but the cowboy who'd just walked out of the kitchen was way more potent than any expensive bubbly.

She'd blown out the candles and flipped on the overhead, which allowed her to confirm what she'd suspected. The champagne was primo. How Granny had come by such a high-priced bottle was a mystery, but not her reason for trotting it out for this dinner.

Granny wanted this matchup and she wasn't above adding some fermented grape juice to help things along. She needn't have bothered.

Rance's devotion to the older woman had melted the last of Lani's reservations. To think she'd written him off as shallow. He had depths she'd only begun to understand.

A few days ago, she might have assumed he'd invited Granny to live with him simply for research purposes. But that didn't explain the way he'd leaped from the truck when she'd appeared on the porch without a coat. He cherished her.

Granny adored him, too. She'd raced outside because she'd been worried about him.

After only a couple of months, their bond was as strong or stronger than a blood tie.

He must have finished their goodnight chat because he was on his way back. The click of his boots on the cabin's wooden floor made her blood pump faster and her thoughts run in circles. Decision time.

He'd made it clear earlier that the choice was hers. Unless she brought up the subject, they'd do the dishes and he'd drive her home. Under his devil-may-care smile lay a strength of character that she'd totally missed until now.

He paused in the doorway. Dragged in a breath.

Heart pounding, she set the ice bucket on the counter and turned. "What?"

"Granny thinks you're in love with me."

The breath left her lungs in a rush. "Granny's... very perceptive." She gulped in air.

His eyes widened. "She's right?"

"To be clear...." She still couldn't breathe worth a damn. "I've tried... I've tried not to be."

"Tried and failed?" A gleam in his dark eyes, he took a step into the kitchen.

"You haven't been much help."

"Oh?" He kept moving.

"Bringing me over here, letting me see how cute you and Granny are with each other, breaking out the expensive champagne—"

"That wasn't me."

"She just took it upon herself to serve your—"

"It was hers." He was close now, very close. "Mom gave it to her as a welcome present back in

October. She has no idea how much it costs. Please don't tell her."

"I won't." She held his gaze. "It was really good champagne. I can still taste it."

His breath hitched. "Me, too."

Her heart thumped so fast it made her ears buzz. "Please take me to bed."

Heat flared in his eyes. "You've got it." Reaching for her hand, he wove his fingers through hers and tightened his grip. "Come with me." He led her out of the kitchen, flipping off the light as he passed by the switch.

Good thing he had a firm grip on her, because she wasn't exactly steady on her feet. Definitely not the booze, either. She'd been fine clearing the table. "What about the dishes?"

"They'll wait. This won't."

The urgency in his voice tightened the coil of need deep in her core. She ached as she never remembered aching before.

She fought to keep things in perspective. This didn't change anything. Like he'd said before, they'd just have some fun, knowing it couldn't be more than that.

But it already was. She'd admitted to being in love with him. Sort of. Was he in love with her? His actions made it highly likely. But he hadn't said so.

The click of his door closing made her shiver. Drawing her close, he lowered his head, his breath warm against her lips. "Buckle up, Lani-lou."

She opened her mouth to protest that stupid name and he cut her off with a kiss that fried her brain and drenched her panties. Didn't take him long to divest her of those panties, along with every stitch she had on.

She tried to return the favor, but he was a moving target. She'd only managed a few buttons on his shirt before he'd picked her up and laid her on his bed, not bothering to turn back the covers. Not that she needed any.

His hot gaze swept over her, more effective than any blanket. "I imagined this so many times and you're even... you're more beautiful than I ever...." His chest heaved. "Thank you."

"You need to—"

"First things first." Toeing off his boots, he climbed in and gave her a kiss that left her breathless. Then he moved on, exploring and tasting with a brush of his lips here or a swipe of his tongue there.

Each liquid caress suggested his ultimate destination. The warm cotton of his shirt and the soft denim of his jeans brushed her increasingly sensitive skin. When anticipation rose to a fever pitch, he slid down between her thighs and claimed the most intimate kiss of all.

She gulped and clutched handfuls of the comforter as her body began to hum, then tremble, then shake. She was there... *there,* blasting off into space, trailing smoke and fire. Was that her yelling, belting out a string of X-rated words?

Gradually the rocket ride slowed and she settled back to earth, limp and struggling to breathe. The mattress shifted and she opened her eyes.

Rance sat in a chair a few feet away, his gaze on her as he pulled off his socks. "Hey, there."

"Did I…" She cleared her throat. "Did I yell?"

He smiled. "Yes, ma'am." He dropped his socks to the floor and stood.

"Did I swear, too?"

His smiled widened. "Yes, ma'am."

"Oh, my God." Her face heated. "What if Granny—"

"She didn't." He unfastened the rest of his shirt buttons.

"She must have. I was shouting."

"I tested it last night. I turned my music way up, banged pots and pans, sang at the top of my lungs."

"Meanwhile Granny was lying in bed laughing her head off." But she was losing interest in the discussion. He'd just tossed his shirt onto the chair, revealing the muscular chest she'd felt but never seen. Her fingertips tingled.

"I thought of that, so I turned off the music and lights, snuck down the hall and peeked in her room. She was sawing logs."

"She could've been faking."

"I know a fake snore when I hear it." He unfastened his jeans. "This one was real." Hooking his thumbs in the waistband of his briefs, he pushed both briefs and jeans down, stepped out of them and kicked them away.

Concern about Granny's hearing evaporated as Lani focused on something far more compelling. Her core tightened. Evidently the climax he'd given her moments ago hadn't been enough.

Rance's amused chuckle snapped her out of her daze. She glanced up. "Sorry. I was ogling. Not cool."

"Maybe not, but my ego loves it." He opened the bedside table drawer and took out a condom packet. "Now comes the buzzkill."

"Says you."

"No, really." He left the package on the nightstand and rolled on the condom. "I'm glad these exist and I use them faithfully, but they look ridiculous."

"I can make it disappear."

His eyes glittered as he put one knee on the bed and moved over her. "I'm counting on it, saucy lady. I have a hunch you'll make me forget I'm even wearing one."

Rubbing her palms up his lightly furred chest, she held his gaze. "I have a hunch you'll make me forget my name."

"Lani-lou?"

She scratched him lightly with her fingernails. "Watch it, buster."

Leaning down, he brushed his mouth over hers while the tip of his cock nudged the spot he'd loved so thoroughly moments ago. "You like it when I call you that."

Her breath hitched. "No, I don't." Slipping her hands to his waist, she reached around and pressed her fingers into his tight buns.

"I say you do. And now, when you hear it, you'll remember this." He pushed gently, gaining purchase. Then he paused.

"Reconsidering?"

"Savoring."

"Guess the mindless sex machine's off-duty." She tightened her grip.

His glutes flexed beneath her fingers. "Just on a tight leash." He eased in a little more. "We only get one first time, Lani-lou."

She pinched him.

He nuzzled his way to the side of her neck and bit her earlobe.

"Hey."

"Hey, yourself." Lifting his head, he held her gaze.

The emotion shining there mirrored hers. "Are you scared?"

"Terrified."

"Me, too. What if it's really good?"

"I think it's gonna be."

She gulped. "I think you're right. Wanna stop?"

He choked out a laugh. "Stop? Are you crazy?"

"It's an idea. You haven't even—" She gasped as he thrust deep and stayed there. "Wow."

"Yeah." He gulped for air. "I knew it. Perfect."

"My fault. I'm the one who asked you to—"

"Shh." Dipping his head again, he kissed her, sweetly, lingeringly. Then he began to move.

She fell into his rhythm naturally, rising to meet him, pleasure flowing in an undulating stream. Her body was so in tune with his that their breath synchronized, even when they began to gasp and pant as the tension mounted.

Surging toward the waterfall, they plunged over, their cries woven as tightly as their quivering bodies.

Lani had never known anything like it. And there was no going back.

11

Rance firmly believed he and Lani were right for each other, but he hadn't figured on getting the sun, moon and stars on the first try. Might've been a fluke, but he didn't think so.

Instead his fate was sealed. If he couldn't be with Lani, and his chances were slim, he was destined to remain single for the rest of his life.

"You don't look very happy for someone who recently sounded like he was living the dream."

Opening his eyes, he gazed down at her flushed, beautiful face. "I'm happy."

"Then why aren't you smiling?"

"Why aren't you smiling, good-time girl? You were whooping it up right along with me."

"Of course I was. It was good." She heaved a sigh. "Too good."

"Exactly. Want to do it again?" He'd be a fool not to ask, since this might be the one and only time they'd be in this bedroom together.

"What if it's even better? What then, smarty-pants?"

"I'll take that chance, but first we have to regroup. Or I do. You can stay put."

"I'm thirsty."

"Me, too. It's the champagne. But stay there." He left the bed and headed for his bathroom. "I'll take care of things and then get us some water."

"Naked?"

"I'll wrap a towel around me," he called over his shoulder, "but I doubt it's necessary. Granny doesn't get up at night."

"Are you sure about that? My grandma gets up several times a night."

"Okay, maybe she does get up and I just haven't noticed." He stepped into the bathroom.

"She probably does, and unless you modified the floorplan like my folks did, the second bathroom is down the hall."

"You've made your point. I'll put on my jeans."

"I'd offer to get us water, but if she doesn't run into me, she never has to know I stayed."

"She'll know."

"How?"

He finished washing up and walked out. "Because I'll tell her."

"Why do that?" In the interim she'd pulled back the covers and propped herself up with a pillow. She drilled him with a what-the-hell look.

"Guaranteed she'll ask me, and I'm not gonna lie. I promise she won't say anything to anyone. She passed that test by keeping my book a secret since October."

"I guess it doesn't matter if she knows. I'd just rather my family didn't find out."

Sounded like she'd be embarrassed, which nicked his pride. "Afraid your dad will come after me with a shotgun?"

"Don't be ridiculous."

"You're right. He's a peaceful sort. Your mom's more the type to wave that double-barrel at me."

That got her to smile. "She'd have to point it at me. I'm the holdout. You'd probably go along with a shotgun wedding."

"Not if you don't want me." He pulled on his briefs and picked up his jeans.

"That's the problem. I do."

The knot in his chest loosened some. "Thank you for that." He held her gaze. "It means a lot. But you're in love with that publishing house and I refuse to break up a happy relationship." Buttoning and zipping his jeans, he crossed to the door, opened it and stepped out. He almost ran into Granny. "Hey, there."

"Rance! Jaysus! Nearly scared the life out of me, ya did."

"Sorry." He quickly closed the door behind him. "Just got up to fetch a glass of water."

"What didja say?"

"I NEED A GLASS OF WATER!" Technically he needed two, but he chose not to be that specific.

"Ah. 'Tis what I'm after, too. My throat's drier than Maeve O'Malley's soda bread. Ya never tasted somethin' that dry. Like chewin' on a brick." She tightened the sash on her robe as she walked toward the dark kitchen, her slippers whispering over the wooden floor. Whoops. They'd left the place a mess. "SORRY ABOUT THE DISHES!"

"Broke 'em in a fit of passion, didja?"

"WE LEFT WITHOUT CLEANING UP!"

"Well, good on ya. How's it goin', then?"

"GREAT!"

"Grand was it?" She paused and turned back to him. "Fer both a ya? Lani, too?"

His face heated. Good thing he was hidden by the shadows. "For both of us."

"Ya hafta repeat that, lad. M'ears are in m'bedroom."

Might as well cut to the chase. "SHE'S HAD TWO ORGASMS SO FAR!"

"Fair play, boyo! Had to check. Tis always grand fer the fella, y'know. Ya have ta give her a good time, too."

"I PROMISE I WILL!"

"Good. Ya be needin' ta stay hydrated, then." She spun around and made for the kitchen.

When she flipped on the light she didn't spare a glance for the dishes stacked on the counter. Taking three large glasses from the cupboard, she quickly filled them from the tap and handed him two.

"Thanks." Even if she couldn't hear that, she'd probably read his lips.

"You're welcome." She flapped her hands at him. "Go on, now. Keep it up."

He choked back a laugh as he left the kitchen. She hadn't meant it the way his lust-filled brain had heard it. Or maybe she had.

He'd worried that he'd shock her with the explicit sex scenes in his book. She might be more informed on the subject than he was.

Would Lani be mad at him for his detailed answer to Granny's question? Clearly that was the info she'd been after. She should have given him more credit. Then again, she hadn't read his book yet.

Lani greeted him with a big grin. Not mad at him.

"I'm glad you thought it was funny."

"I just wish I hadn't left my phone in my tote. I would have stood by the door and recorded it."

"For what? Blackmail?" He passed over a glass of water and set his on the nightstand so he could shuck his jeans.

"No, just for me."

"A souvenir? Something to remember me by in your twilight years?" He wanted to spend those years with her, which was probably why he'd said it, pressing on a tender place in his heart to see how bad it hurt. He climbed into bed.

"I won't have any trouble remembering you."

"I can't tell if that's a compliment or not."

"It's simply a fact. You're not going anywhere and my whole family is here. We'll see each other at least once a year, probably twice, for the rest of our lives."

He stared at her. How had he managed to ignore that eventuality?"

"You haven't thought about that, have you?"

"No, damn it. Have you?"

"Not until you said that thing about twilight years." She held his gaze. "And guess what? I'll probably spend mine right here."

"In my bed?"

"This isn't a joke. You know what I mean. Here. On Rowdy Ranch."

"Aw, hell. Are you saying you'll *retire* out here?"

"It's logical. I don't see Kieran and Sara going anywhere. My folks look healthier than they have in ages. They might still be around, too."

"So I don't stand a chance now, but in forty years, it'll be clear sailing?"

"It's not funny, damn it."

"Ironic, though, if after all that time, we finally... well, unless you have a husband, in which case...." The nightmare scenario took a turn for the worse. "You'll not only bring him when you retire, you'll drag him to the ranch every blessed time you visit."

"And even more fun, I'll get to know whoever you're with."

Denial rose in his throat. He tried to swallow it, which resulted in a caveman grunt of dismissal. Not particularly attractive.

"I don't like thinking about you with someone else, but I'd better get used to the idea. Some lucky lady will be enjoying all this." She swept a hand around the room. "Your packed bookshelves, your cute little tree by the fireplace. Is it real?"

"The tree's real. The fireplace is electric." Leaning toward the nightstand, he opened the drawer.

Her breath hitched.

"I'm getting the remote for the fireplace."

"Oh."

"But I'd be happy to grab a condom while I'm at it."

"Don't let me stop you."

He looked over his shoulder. "You could, you know. After what we just discussed, you'd be smart to cut your losses."

"Do you want to?"

"No."

"Neither do I."

"Alrighty, then." He tossed a condom on the nightstand and picked up the remote. "But first, some atmosphere. Do you like crackling logs, glowing embers or something in between?"

"Can I play with it?"

"You can play with anything in this room, including me." He handed over the remote.

"I'll keep that in mind." She pointed the remote at the fireplace and went through the settings. "I'm in the mood for this one — gentle flames so you get a flicker but it's not loud."

"Good choice. Want music?"

She smiled. "You have a remote for that?"

"Yes, and before you ding me for my seductive setup—"

"I wasn't gonna." She picked up her water and settled back against the pillows.

"But you were thinking it."

"Maybe."

"Ninety percent of the time I'm alone in here. Since February, it's been a hundred percent. Just me and my laptop."

"You write in here?"

"A lot, yeah. During the day I sometimes sit at my old rolltop desk. I have a great view of the Sapphires from that window." He took several swallows of water.

"But there's no door to close. And now you have Granny here."

"That lady's amazingly quiet. Never interrupts me, except for the time a bear strolled past the cabin two days after she moved in. But you make a good point. I sink into the story more when I'm in here with my music on and the door closed."

"And surrounded by books. I think you have more than me."

"That's not even all of them. I enclosed my back porch for a workout room and I put up shelves in there to handle the overflow."

She gave his chest the kind of appraisal guaranteed to get a rise out of him. "I figured you must work out."

"Not as much as I used to. I'd rather write than sweat."

"This is you on a reduced exercise regime?"

Evidently the muscles he had were enough. That was gratifying. "A year ago I could bench press two-twenty. Bulking up was my strategy for impressing women."

"Did it work?"

"Like a charm. But I've switched strategies. Now I write books."

"To impress women?"

"One woman." Tilting back his head, he drank the rest of the water and set the glass on the nightstand.

Her gaze sharpened. "You said you didn't write *Tequila Shots* for me."

"I didn't." He picked up the condom, one more step down the path to nowhere. "I wrote it for us."

12

I wrote it for us. Rance's confession blasted through her sensual mood and gave her a harsh slap of reality. What was she doing here?

Every moment she spent in his bed was a cheat. She wasn't his one true love, despite the fantasies he'd built. Time to get the hell out of here before she did any more damage to his dreams.

Putting down her water glass, she scooted around so she was facing him. God, he was beautiful. She ached for his touch, but she couldn't keep selfishly taking what he offered. Lovely though it was.

His gaze clouded. "Clearly I shouldn't have admitted that."

"I'm glad you did. There is no *us* but I get why you believed there would be. Now it's time to be smart and cut—"

"Wish I'd swallowed that comment, too. Me and my big mouth."

His very kissable, talented mouth. "But you're right. We—"

"Mom says I'm overly verbal. I need to talk less and think—"

"Rance, this isn't your fault."

"Feels like it."

"I didn't see forty years into the future, either."

"I did, but it was a different movie."

She covered his hand, the one that held the condom. "Seriously, we need to cut our losses."

Foil crinkled as he closed his fist. "Taking you home before we use this seems like we're adding to our losses."

"It's wrong for me to enjoy your body while shoving a knife in your heart."

He blinked. "You're feeling guilty?"

"Of course I am. I let myself get carried away by your book, your cozy cabin, your sexy body. When all along I knew we'd never—"

"Whoa, whoa." Leaving the condom on the mattress, he took both her hands in his. "I wrote the book. I kissed you. I invited you here. I suggested we could fool around after dinner. If anyone should feel guilty, it's me."

"There's nothing wrong with making a play for the woman you've fallen for. But I—"

"You fell for me, too." His grip tightened. "There's also nothing wrong with wanting to make love with the man you've fallen for. Give yourself a break for being human, Lani-lou."

She gulped. "I...I need to tell you something. I don't hate that nickname."

"I know. And it's not just a nickname. It's an endearment."

His soft tone and the warm light in his dark eyes made her throat hurt.

"I care about you so much that I need to call you something that no one else does. And when you show up with that husband you're gonna find, I intend to call you Lani-lou right in front of him."

Her breath caught. "You're giving up?"

"That would be dumb, wouldn't it? We're just four days away from Christmas. I've been very good this year and Santa knows what I want. That ol' boy might just find a way to give me what I asked for."

"You believe in Santa?"

"Yes, ma'am." He said it with complete seriousness, without a hint of a smile or a twinkle of mischief in his eyes. "Don't you?"

"I guess I... sort of do."

That got a smile out of him. "I'll make allowances for that lukewarm endorsement. You're a city girl and this is your first country Christmas. Trust me, it's easier to believe in Santa when you're surrounded by pine trees and starry skies."

"That I can totally agree with."

He took a deep breath. "I'm about to break a promise."

Her heart thumped faster. "I can guess which one."

"Please don't make me take you home. Let's wait for the fire to die down."

"It's an electric fireplace."

"That's not the fire I'm referring to."

"I know." Leaning forward, she brushed her mouth against his. "Your mom's right. You need to talk less."

With a soft groan, he let go of her hands, cupped her head and held her still. His warm breath tickled her lips. "Thank you."

Then he began making sweet love to her mouth. He took his time building the tension, teasing her with nibbles and licks. Gradually the moist press of his lips grew more urgent. Pressing his fingers into her scalp, he tilted her head back and shifted to his knees, ravishing her with deep thrusts of his tongue.

Without touching her anywhere else, he created havoc in her trembling, aching body. But she could touch him... anywhere. Instinctively she reached for what she craved.

When she wrapped both hands around his solid length and squeezed, he gasped and lifted his lips a fraction from hers. "Careful."

"You said I could play with anything in this room."

"I don't want to come."

"Then don't." She swept her thumb over the sensitive tip, making him shudder.

"I'm...out of practice."

Because he'd been celibate for months, saving himself for her. "Then I'll find the condom." She kept one hand on the object of her desire while she patted the mattress in search of the small package. "Got it."

"Let me." He reached for it.

She put it behind her back. "I want to. I'll be quick." Or as quick as she could be when she was shaking with excitement.

She yearned to take on the intimate task. Since she'd chosen to make love with him one more time, she was determined to etch every moment with significance.

His breath hissed through his teeth when she started rolling it on, so she moved faster. "That's it. You're suited up."

"Thank God." Spanning her waist with both hands, he lifted her off the bed.

She clutched his shoulders as he repositioned her. He didn't exactly toss her to the mattress, but she bounced just a wee bit. "Impatient, are we?"

"Sorry."

"Don't be. I'm yours for the taking."

His eyes glittered as he moved between her thighs, his breath coming fast. "I..." He closed his mouth. Shook his head.

"What?"

"Nothing."

His intense gaze warned her to let it go. She did, sliding her arms around his solid body and stroking his back. As he lowered his hips, she spread her fingers over his warm skin, absorbing the flex of his muscles.

Anticipation hummed through her veins as the blunt tip of his cock nudged her and found purchase. She was so ready to begin this sensual dance of matching rhythms carrying them to a glorious mutual climax.

With a deep-throated sound that was almost a growl, he drove home. And stayed there, panting, his eyes closed.

Her body heat shot up as a spasm rocked her core. She gulped. Another one. Too soon!

He opened his eyes to reveal the fire blazing there. "You're coming." His voice was ragged.

She sucked in a breath. "Uh-huh." Another spasm hit. Soon. Very soon, damn it. "I can't... hold back."

"Don't try." He began to thrust.

And she was lost, helpless to control the eager response of her needy body. "Come with me!"

"No." He stroked with devastating skill. "Go with it, Lani-lou! Show me what you've got!"

She showed him, all right. Yelling like never in her life, she welcomed a climax so powerful she almost blacked out.

He kept moving, prolonging the incredible sensations as he gradually slowed the pace. Then he paused, still firmly seated and fully erect.

She gazed up at him, certain he'd see the adoration in her eyes. "I think you found my G-spot."

"Could be."

Yeah, the gleam in his eyes said he was mighty proud of himself. "You said you were out of practice. But you didn't—"

"Figured out that if I let go, I'd have to take you home."

"I didn't want to come so soon. I liked it when we climaxed together."

"We still can."

"After that orgasmathon? Forget it. I'm tapped out."

"You just think you are." He rocked his hips in a lazy motion. "How's that?"

"Feels nice, but I'm not—oh!" She'd been fixated on the glow in his dark eyes. Meanwhile he'd slipped his hand between her thighs. He had a very talented thumb.

"More interested, now?"

Amazingly, her relaxed core began to tighten. "Against all odds."

His mouth curved in a smile. "Attagirl."

"Showoff. Balancing on one arm." She was dazzled, aroused, and in the market for another Rance-inspired orgasm.

"One-handed pushups. So worth the time."

"Don't get cocky." Her breath hitched as her thighs began to quiver.

"Because you hate that."

"I do."

"Liar." He was breathing harder, now. He'd picked up the pace, too. "Time to bring it on home, Lani-lou." Propped up on both arms again, he held her gaze. "You with me?"

She gasped as the first tremor rolled through her core. "Yes."

"Didn't hear you." He pumped faster.

"Yes!"

"Still didn't hear you!"

"*Yes*!" The dam broke. Pleasure flooded her body as Rance, bellowing in triumph, pushed deep and came with her, his cock pulsing in time with the waves of her climax.

He'd managed to create a spectacular finale to their evening. They could end things on a high note, resist the urge to repeat this behavior and act like rational adults for the rest of the holiday.

Then, in a private moment before she flew back to New Jersey, they'd vow to stay friends as they navigated the next forty, fifty or sixty years.

Yay.

13

He'd gotten more than he'd expected. Rance kept telling himself that as he and Lani put on their clothes, mostly in silence. Before they'd left the bed she'd thanked him for a wonderful time. He'd thanked her for staying for a second round.

After that, conversation had been brief and stilted. He couldn't say what he was thinking, that they needed to find more such opportunities this holiday.

That idea had to come from her, right? Clearly she hadn't leaped to that conclusion or she would have said so by now. She was likely still in the mindset that continuing to have sex would make their future dealings even more impossible.

That could be true. It could be untrue. Nobody could accurately predict the future, could they? Why give up present pleasure when the future of a relationship was still a big fat question mark?

But if he brought up the prospect of more alone time, he might start an argument and ruin the evening they'd just enjoyed. He was incredibly lucky to have spent this time with her, and if that was all he ever had….

Oh, to hell with it. He didn't care for that self-defeating crap. She'd be here until New Year's Day. That was a long damn time to have her within reach while lecturing himself to be grateful for what he'd had. He wasn't that noble.

He finished buttoning his shirt and tucked it into the waistband of his jeans. "I've been thinking."

"So that's why smoke's coming out your ears."

"You're a funny lady."

"Just trying to keep the mood light." She pulled her red sweater over her head.

He'd enjoyed taking it off. Soft as a baby blanket, but her skin was even softer.

"Don't look at me like that."

"How am I looking at you?"

"You know perfectly well. It's your smolder."

"I've never smoldered in my life."

"Ha. You do it all the time."

"And you hate that, too."

"No. That's why you need to stop."

"Yes, ma'am." He glanced away. "I have an idea."

"Saw that coming." She ran her fingers through her hair. "I haven't checked the time. What—"

"Almost midnight."

"Good. My parents will be asleep. Ready to go?"

"Right after I run this idea past you."

She crossed her arms. "Okay." Her body language said it all. She'd literally armed herself against him.

He'd tell her anyway, let the thought simmer in her brain... and her body. "I said I'd announce the book to the gang on Christmas Day, but there are advantages to spreading the word tomorrow. First we tell Mom and Andy like we planned. Then I send out a group text to everybody else."

"That doesn't sound like you. I'd expect that low-key approach from Lucky or Cheyenne."

"I'd love to see their faces when they get the news, but I'll gladly give up that moment for the chance to be alone with you again."

"Huh?"

"It's baked into the concept, but I didn't see that before. You're my editor. Before you give the manuscript to your boss, you have suggestions for strengthening the conflict."

"Ah." Her eyes darkened and she sucked in a breath, but her arms stayed crossed. "Brainstorming sessions."

"Chaperoned brainstorming sessions. Perfectly legit. No one needs to know what goes on in those sessions but you, me, and Granny."

"You're the most devious man I've ever met."

"Thank you."

"You know in your heart it's a terrible idea."

"Not true. My heart likes it a lot. So does my—"

"Never mind. My answer is no. I actually do have a couple of small suggestions, but I'll put them in an email."

"That's ridiculous. I'm right here."

"I'm aware of that. Very aware."

"We're looking at years and years of not having sex with each other. Please don't throw away this golden opportunity. I don't know why I didn't think of it sooner."

"I do. You figured once I read the book we'd live happily ever after. You didn't expect to be grasping at straws."

"You're much more fun to cuddle than a straw, Lani-lou."

She let out a sigh. "This isn't getting us anywhere. You'd better take me home."

"Oh, it might get us somewhere. I'm sending the group text, regardless of your decision. You'll have several days to think it over. If you change your mind, and I'm gonna bet you do, you know where to find me."

She shook her head. "You're impossible."

"And that's why you love me." Her startled gasp told him he'd hit a nerve. He hadn't meant to. "Sorry. That's my automatic response when somebody says I'm impossible. I've been called that a lot."

"Listen, Rance, I—"

"Hey, we're dealing with some complicated emotions. Falling for each other isn't the same as making a commitment. I didn't mean to imply you had. Like I said. Knee-jerk reaction."

"We should leave."

"Yes, we should." He gestured for her to go out ahead of him.

As he followed her into the living room and helped her on with her coat, he resisted the urge to massage his chest, which was tight as a drum and hurt like hell.

Nice little speech he'd made, but it didn't change what he'd seen in her eyes when he'd come out with that flippant comment. She wasn't just falling. She was there. In love. With him.

That was what he'd wanted, right? And he'd succeeded brilliantly. Congrats to him. How was she supposed to go find that husband now? As things stood, he'd just handed her a bucketful of suffering.

Unless he was willing to let her carry it for months, maybe years, he'd better come up with a solution to this mess. And do it fast. The problem required a permanent fix, something more consequential than a few stolen hours in each other's arms.

He'd find it or die trying. Well, he wouldn't literally *die.* But if he brought long-term sorrow to the woman he loved, he might as well be dead.

14

Evidently good sex won out over anxiety. Lani slept until her alarm went off and woke up feeling terrific. She'd love to have Rance lying next to her. Then she could roll over and... yikes, not the thoughts she should be having if she intended to pull up the gangplank.

She would do that, right? She'd told him no and she'd stick with that. But she couldn't wait to see him again.

Glancing at her phone, she hopped out of bed. She had just enough time to shower, dress in something cute and grab a quick breakfast before he arrived at nine.

Her shower went fast but choosing an outfit took longer. Yeah, she wanted to look good for Rance. That had been true since she'd met the guy back in February. She just hadn't admitted it.

The clingy gold sweater she chose emphasized her breasts and the gold flecks in her eyes. Although she'd tried to think of ways he could mute his sexiness, he hadn't asked the same of her.

That said, a woman determined to hold the line had no business wearing this sweater. Turned out the woman gazing back at her as she put on her makeup was seriously considering his latest tantalizing scheme.

No matter how hard she'd worked to keep him at arm's length he'd managed to sneak past her defenses. His book had severely weakened them and last night had finished the job.

If his prediction that he'd be a letdown in the sack compared to Dooley had been true, she might have saved herself. Saved him, too, because she wasn't the only one facing heartbreak.

But his lovemaking hadn't been a letdown. Far from it. He'd been... she paused, her mascara wand halfway to her flushed face, her body tingling and her breath wonky. He'd been so damn....

She gulped as a wave of lust left her shaking. Better stop thinking about it before she stabbed herself in the eye with the wand. Besides, she had to get some breakfast and announce her plans to her folks without alerting them to... anything.

She'd hoped they might be out of the kitchen by the time she walked in, but no such luck. Instead they were lingering over a second cup of coffee and evidently feeling chatty.

And curious, at least in her mom's case. She asked what Granny had served for dinner. Oh, no. They'd forgotten the pound cake. Shoot.

She briefly described the meal and apologized for not bringing a couple of slices back with her. "Everything was delicious." She hoped she'd said that with the right amount of enthusiasm — not too little and not too much.

"I'm sure it was." Her sweet dad didn't suspect a thing. He never did. "Granny's a hoot. Fits in like she was born here."

"She does. Well, I gotta run. Rance and I are heading over to the ranch house in a few minutes." She washed down her peanut butter toast with a few swallows of coffee. "He's picking me up."

Her mother's brows arched. "Another sleigh ride?"

"No, something else. Christmas secrets."

"Say no more, sweetheart." Her dad grinned. "This Christmas will be one for the record books. I still can't believe we cut down our own tree. Or that we'll ride down Main Street in a sleigh and the next day have almost thirty for Christmas dinner at Desiree's."

"Maybe more. When you start with ten—" Thunder's distinctive rumble wiped out all thoughts but one. "That'll be Rance." Heart racing, she left the table and carried her dishes to the sink.

Her dad stood. "I'll get the door."

"Thanks, Dad. Tell him I'll be right there." She put her mug and plate in the dishwasher.

"I take it you had a nice time last night."

She kept her expression neutral as she turned to face her mom. "I did."

"I wondered how it would go, since you two don't always get along. But since you're taking off with him this morning you must have ironed out your differences."

"We have." She did her best to keep a straight face. That meant ignoring the sound of Rance's voice in the entryway, which gave her goosebumps. She chose her words carefully. "Since we'll be seeing each other a few times a year, we might as well be friends."

"I hope that's possible. You probably know he has a crush on you."

What the hell could she say to that? "Well, I—"

"Hey, guess what?" Her dad strode into the kitchen carrying a glass container with a snap-on lid. "We have pound cake, after all!"

Rance followed him, all smiles. "Good morning, ladies! I realized after I brought Lani home last night that this hadn't made the trip." He gestured toward the container. "It spent the night in my truck so I wouldn't forget a second time."

"Thanks, Rance." Her mom beamed at him. "Very considerate of you."

"The credit goes to Granny. She put in the work. I'm just the unreliable delivery boy. You were supposed to have it with your breakfast. My apologies."

"No worries, son." Her dad clapped him on the shoulder. "I noticed the snow's picked up. I see a cozy fire and a mid-morning snack in my future."

"It's snowing?" Lani glanced toward the window above the sink where she'd been standing moments ago. She'd been so focused on navigating the interior landscape she'd been blind to the flakes swirling outside.

"Yes, ma'am." Rance's eyes twinkled with amusement. "You'd best bundle up."

Although there was nothing inherently suggestive in any of that, her heart stuttered and her cheeks grew warm. Not good. "I left my scarf in my room. I'll be back in a sec." She hurried past him.

Had her folks heard his soft, sexy chuckle? She sure hoped not.

Since she didn't plan to be out in the snow, she didn't need the scarf but she'd wanted a chance to brush her teeth and put on lipstick. On the way back to the kitchen, she detoured past the entry, grabbed her coat and slipped it on.

In her absence, Rance had taken a seat at the kitchen table. Coat unbuttoned and hat on his lap, he looked right at home as her folks shared their tree-chopping adventure.

She hadn't been around for it since they'd decided to do the deed before she arrived and surprise her. Sara had texted her about the incident, starting out with *The good news is Mom was not killed by a Christmas tree.*

"I've never seen Vanessa move that fast." Her dad shook his head. "I don't know how we miscalculated the angle, but she was smack-dab in the path of it. And she leaped out of the way like an elite athlete. Impressive."

"Until I lost my balance and fell in a snowbank."

"Better than having a seventy-pound tree land on you." Her dad glanced up as she walked in. "Next year we'll wait for you to get here, sweetheart. Chopping your own tree sure does jumpstart the Christmas spirit."

"Yeah." Her mom laughed. "Not to mention the adrenaline rush when you're almost KO'd as it comes crashing down."

"I admire your grit," Rance said, "but just remember I'm available if you ever want some help."

"Appreciate it," her dad said with a grin, "but we enjoy screwing up these things on our own."

"Alrighty, then. I totally understand." He looked over at her. "We'd better get going."

"Yep. Before the snow gets any worse."

"We'll be fine." He picked up his hat by its crown and stood. "Thunder can handle it." In a move that was all cowboy, he put on the hat and tugged down the brim.

A simple thing, but she found it mesmerizing. Always had. Cowboys. Who knew?

"We're off." He gestured for her to go ahead of him.

"Thanks for the pound cake," her mom called after them.

"You're welcome," he called back. On the way through the living room he glanced at the sizeable tree in the corner. "I'm glad your mom is nimble."

"So am I. Evidently they had many offers of help, but they were determined to do it by themselves."

"I'm all for folks doing for themselves. More power to 'em." He ushered her out the front door and quickly closed it behind them.

Thunder was parked horizontally right by the steps with the passenger door facing her. Good thing her folks hadn't put in a walkway yet.

"You do know you just contradicted yourself by opening the door for me when I was perfectly capable of doing it myself."

He sighed. "Are you still having trouble with cowboy manners, Lani-lou?"

"No." She turned and flashed him a smile. "I just said that to get a rise out of you."

"Doesn't take much." Slinging an arm around her shoulders, he hustled her down the steps as snow whipped around them. "That gold sweater does the trick. And you're flirting with me." Opening the door, he gave her a hand up. "If I didn't know better, I'd think you're sending me a signal."

"Against my better judgment."

"I like the sound of that." He closed the door and jogged around to the driver's side. Once in, he started the motor before fastening his seat belt. Thunder beeped at him. "Yeah, yeah. Gotta keep the lady warm, buddy."

She ducked her head to hide a smile. Rance talked to his truck. One more adorable trait added to a growing list.

He buckled up, switched on the wipers and put Thunder in gear.

"Did you remember the two manuscripts?"

"Damn, I knew there was something I was supposed to bring."

"Don't tell me you forgot the most important part of—"

He grinned. "They're in a box behind my seat."

"Are they mine and Granny's?"

"I got up early and printed out another one so Granny can keep hers. Now let's hear what's going on in that top-notch brain of yours."

"I think you fried it. I can't stop thinking about last night."

"Join the club. It's a wonder I remembered to bring those manuscripts considering I forgot to put water in the coffee pot this morning."

"Oh, no!"

"It was okay after it cooled off. But then I burned the eggs I was making for Granny and me, and I never burn eggs. When the toaster began smoking, she sent me out of the kitchen and took over making breakfast."

"Wow. Are you safe to drive?"

He grinned. "I guess we'll see."

"You're in worse shape than me. Pull over. I'll drive."

"Much as I'd love to watch you take the wheel, a snowstorm isn't the best time for your first experience."

"I know, but—"

"Don't worry, we'll get there just fine. It's not far and Thunder knows the way."

"Sure he does." She peered out the windshield as the wipers swished rapidly back and forth. "It's really coming down. Could we get stuck at your mom's place?"

"Not for long. We have plows. We even have one I can hook up to Thunder if I need to."

"I don't suppose you have it with you."

"No, but Sky could use it with his truck if he had to. It won't be necessary, though."

"When are you scheduled to work?"

"Eleven to five again, but if it keeps snowing like this, that might change. Enough about the weather." He paused. Took a deep breath. "Do we have a date tonight?"

"Oh!" She began to quiver. "Well, um…" Her voice shook, too. She wasn't prepared to make that decision. She'd thought they'd discuss their options later in the day with a few kisses thrown in. Nope.

She wanted to be with him again. But a second rendezvous, especially so soon, would deepen their connection.

"It's yes or no time. I need to let Granny know about dinner, because if you won't be there, she'll set up another afternoon tea with Marybeth."

"Are we messing up Granny's social life?"

"I asked. We're her number one priority."

"I assume she knows I won't be relocating."

"She does."

"What does she say to that?"

"She thinks you'd be crazy to let me get away."

"Ah."

"This is our last chance for a while. Tomorrow night's the caroling thing. The next night's Christmas Eve."

She gulped. "I see your point."

"And?"

She knew this sensation. It was like standing at the edge of the high-dive board gathering her courage to jump. "Yes. My answer is yes."

"Hot damn."

<u>15</u>

Live for the moment. That was Rance's plan and he was sticking to it. In this moment he was driving though a considerable snowstorm with very important passengers — Lani and two copies of his manuscript.

Maybe he should also count Dooley and Sophia, his partners in this journey. Dooley, Sophia and Granny had helped pave the way to Lani's decisive *yes* just now.

Now that she'd agreed to spend a few more hours making love with him, he was wary of saying anything more in case it was the wrong thing. He just drove, using his inner GPS more than his eyes.

His mother's turnoff should be... here. He eased the truck to the right and prayed he wouldn't knock down the modest sign marking her road.

"How did you know to turn? I can't see a thing."

"Thunder told me."

"Well, that certainly explains it."

"I know these roads. I've driven them so many times I've bragged that I could do it blindfolded. I guess I can, because I can't see anything, either."

"We're on a road, though. We'd feel it if we were out in the pasture."

"It's her road. I'm sure of it. We're about to go around the bend and she'll have all her lights on so we can see the house."

"And not run into it?"

"That would be preferable."

"And you know where the bend is?"

"Thunder does."

"Uh-huh."

"Here we go." He swung slowly to the right again, taking the curve his gut told him was under the tires. If he got stuck in a ditch driving blind like an idiot, he'd never hear the end of it.

"Lights! I see them! Not very bright because they're blocked by the snow, but that's the house. You did it." She sank back against the seat.

"I'll probably get a lecture."

"Why?"

"Mom sent me a text just as I was pulling into your folks' place. She said if it got worse she wanted me to hold up there and reschedule this discussion."

"But it didn't get worse until we were on our way."

"That's what I say. She might see it differently."

"But you didn't want to put this off."

"No, ma'am, I did not."

"Understood. I'll back you up. It wasn't that bad when we left, and then we had no choice but to keep going."

"Sounds perfectly rational to me." He inched his way up to the house, getting as close to the porch as he dared. Even grazing it would wipe out his credibility. Pushing gently on the brake, he brought Thunder to a stop and switched off the engine.

"We're here." She sounded relieved.

"I didn't mean to scare you."

"I wasn't scared. Not too much, anyway, and we needed to get here. Telling her about the book is a big deal."

"It is, in more ways than one. Yikes, here comes Andy."

Wearing a heavy parka with the fur-lined hood up, his mom's beloved husband made his way down the steps. Head down, he started toward the truck, a bundle in his arms, like a Saint Bernard with a keg of brandy. Or in this case, the Rescue Quilt.

Rance unfastened his seat belt. "Stay here. I'll go meet him." Hopping down, he closed the door and clamped his hand on his hat as he started toward Andy. The wind was vicious, turning the snow into thousands of tiny needles.

"Looks like you have the Rescue Quilt!"

"I do!"

"Thank you!" He wouldn't have thought it necessary, but now that he was out in the storm, he was grateful, especially for Lani's sake. He moved faster so Andy wouldn't have so far to go.

When they met, Rance took the old familiar quilt. "I appreciate this. Lani will, too."

"Glad you made it, son." Turning, he battled his way back to the porch steps.

Rance watched until he got there okay before heading around to Thunder's passenger door, one hand gripping the quilt and the other securing his hat. He had to squeeze between the front bumper and the porch. Another foot and he would have banged into it.

The heavy patchwork quilt under his arm had started out on his mother's bed long before he was born. When she'd upgraded to a comforter, this handmade treasure had been passed down through the siblings. He and Lucky had traded off weekly until Angie had come along.

After Angie moved out, it had become known as the Rescue Quilt, deployed whenever someone needed extra protection during a major snowstorm. Like if someone got stranded in the barn. More often it was a courtesy provided when a visitor would have trouble making it from their vehicle to the front door without turning into an icicle.

He had no illusions. This gesture was meant for Lani. If he'd been alone, the Rescue Quilt would still be in the hall closet. His mom believed in consequences for actions taken contrary to her wishes.

He opened Lani's door and flipped one side of the quilt up over the door frame. It was padded wool and heavy enough to stay put. "Andy brought this so we could get under it while we make our way to the porch."

"What a nice thing to do. Your mom must not be upset with you."

"Oh, I think she is. Trust me, this is for your benefit, not mine." Holding the edge of the quilt with one hand, he helped her down with the other.

She'd put on her gloves. Smart move. He hadn't bothered and his hands ached from the cold.

"I'm down. Now what?"

"I'll unhook that side from the doorframe and give it to you. Hold it over your head and stick close to me. We'll be better off going around the tailgate."

"G-got it."

"Sorry, Lani. We should have stayed—"

"Nope. You did the right thing."

"Thanks." Maintaining his hold on one end, he slipped the other end free of the door and transferred it to her. Then he slammed the door and lifted his side of the quilt over his head. "Let's go."

Huddled under it, they made a herky-jerky dash for the porch and managed to climb the steps without losing the quilt or their balance.

Lani stood there gasping for breath. "Oh, my God. That was crazy, but it worked better than I expected."

The heavy wooden door opened. "Get in here, you two." His mom beckoned to them. "Rance McLintock, I swear. You—"

"I know, Mom. It would have been smarter to stay at Vanessa and Harry's." He glanced down at Sam, who stood wagging his tail like crazy. "You would know better than that, wouldn't you, pup?"

"He would have. Give me the quilt. I'll drape it over the kitchen chairs so it can dry."

He lifted it off Lani's shoulders, then his. "I can take it—"

"You'll track water on the kitchen floor. Both of you get out of your coats and boots and skedaddle into the living room. Andy's got a nice fire going."

Yeah, she was ticked. He helped Lani with her coat and hooked it on the rack in the entry. It wasn't until he hung up his own along with his hat that he realized a key element was missing.

He lowered his voice as he toed off his boots. "We left the box in the truck."

"Oh, no. We did, didn't we?"

"Just as well. We might have dropped it in the snow."

"You guys want coffee or hot chocolate?" his mother called from the kitchen.

"Hot chocolate," he called back. "And I'll help make it." He glanced at Lani. "Granny's is good, but Mom's is even more amazing."

"Sounds great. I can help, too, unless…"

"Yeah, better let me. I need to, if you get my drift."

"I do. Sam and I will go check out Andy's fire. Holler if you need backup."

He chuckled. "Okay." He walked through the arched doorway into the kitchen.

His mom had begun heating the homemade combo of cocoa, sugar and water that formed the base for her famous hot chocolate. "You can get me the milk and take out some mugs."

He pulled a jug from the fridge and set it on the counter next to the stove. "Driving in this weather was stupid, but I—"

"It was stupid, full stop. Just because you're on ranch roads doesn't mean you couldn't have serious problems. It's one thing to take chances by yourself, but you had Lani with you."

"I did." Guilt washed over him. "There's no excuse for putting her in danger." What if he'd miscalculated on those turns? Hit a jagged rock and punctured a tire? They wouldn't have died, but he would have created a problem, required an elaborate rescue and caused everyone to worry.

"I texted Vanessa when you pulled in. They're very relieved you made it."

"I'll apologize to them." He lined up four mugs on the counter. He'd allowed his focus on a goal to override responsibility to a loved one. He owed Lani a huge apology, too.

"I hope this discussion is important, because if it's some minor—"

"It's not minor." Didn't mean he'd easily forgive himself, though.

"Are you and Lani involved?"

His breath caught. Of course she'd jump to that conclusion. "It's not what you think." Which was true. She likely thought they had a personal announcement to make. Sadly, they did not. But they were involved.

"You're nuts about her." She stirred in the milk.

"I am."

"But you're not here to discuss your relationship?"

"No, ma'am."

"Okay, then. You can reveal whatever it is when we're gathered by the fire. But before we leave the kitchen, I need to tell you something. You deserve to hear it in private so you have a chance to process it."

"What the hell?" His heart jerked in his chest. Her solemn tone meant bad news. "Are you sick? Are you and Andy—"

"No, no. We're both disgustingly healthy and still madly in love. It's—"

"Buck? Marybeth?"

"Calm down, son. This has nothing to do with someone you love. In fact, it's someone you don't much care for. Neither do I, for that matter."

"Then why is it important?"

"Your father called this morning. He's arriving tomorrow."

16

Had Desiree been that tough on Rance? Lani couldn't think of any other reason for the haunted expression in his eyes. He'd smiled when he'd brought in the tray of hot chocolate, but the smile had held no warmth.

The mugs topped with festive swirls of whipped cream and chocolate sprinkles presented a stark contrast to Rance as he put the tray on the coffee table and sat down next to her. When Sam came over for a treat, he fished one out of his pocket and absent-mindedly gave it to him.

The collie took his dog cookie over to his bed, as if knowing his normally affectionate friend wasn't in the mood to pet him. Rance's body radiated tension and his fingers curled as if he longed to make a fist and punch something.

Andy grimaced. "She told you. That's why the hot chocolate took so long."

"I needed to give him time to swear and stomp around." Desiree laid down a plate of Christmas cookies and a pile of napkins on the coffee table. Then she glanced at Lani. "Irving Quick, aka Rance's father, is coming tomorrow and staying through Christmas."

Lani stared at her, the hot chocolate forgotten. "Irving Quick, the thriller writer?"

"Yes."

She turned to Rance. "And you didn't tell me?"

"Why would I? He's not my father. Well, technically he is, but I don't claim him."

Irving Quick was Rance's dad. Wow. What did she know about the guy? Not much except his picture on the dust jacket of his latest hardcover release.

He was photogenic, a broad-shouldered man in a black turtleneck and leather jacket, his dark hair graying at the temples and a cocky smile on his handsome face. She knew that smile. "He'll be staying here?"

"That's the only good news. Mom told him he'd have to find something in town. Unfortunately, he did."

"It should have been impossible at this late date." Desiree picked up one of the mugs and took her favorite easy chair to the right of the sofa. "I was counting on that. Except he's a lucky jackass. He called back within ten minutes. The hotel was booked but Mrs. J had a last-minute cancellation. He has a room at her B&B."

Andy leaned over and grabbed one of the mugs, a napkin and two cookies. "Could she put a sedative in his coffee?"

"Andy." Desiree sent him a look.

"Notice I didn't say poison. A sedative would be harmless." He sighed. "C'mon, everybody, drink your hot chocolate and eat some sugar. If a spoonful helps, this stuff will make us forget all about Quick-dick."

Desiree made a half-hearted attempt to hide her smile behind her mug. "Stop calling him that. Next thing you know you'll say it in front of our darling grandchildren."

"And all hell will break loose. You're right. I'm just trying to work off my frustration that he's landing in our Christmas like a turd in a punchbowl."

Lani choked back laughter and picked up her mug. Good thing she hadn't just taken a drink.

"He says he's a changed man."

Andy snorted. "Sure he is. He looked like the same arrogant bastard on his latest dust jacket."

Desiree paused, a cookie halfway to her mouth. "You paid attention to that?"

"Hard not to see it while I was quietly redistributing his books during your signing last month up in Missoula."

"Redistributing them how?"

"Oh, some ended up in the cookbook section. I stashed a few in self-help, some in ancient history, where he definitely belongs."

Lani grinned. "Remind me never to tick you off." Then she lifted her mug in Desiree's direction. "Tastes wonderful."

"Thank you." Desiree returned her attention to Andy. "Was this redistribution caper a one-time stunt?"

"I'll take the fifth."

"Obviously not an isolated incident, then. Promise you won't do it if we have Mav and Zach with us. You'll set a bad example."

"That's a good point. I'll pass the word."

"Pass the word? What the hell? You have accomplices?"

"I wouldn't say that. Hey Rance, drink up, son. You don't want to let your mom's famous hot chocolate get cold."

"Right." He leaned forward and took the last mug from the tray.

Desiree continued gazing at Andy. "We need to discuss your clandestine activities, but we can do it later."

His expression remained serene. "Can't wait, my love."

Lani grabbed a cookie and a napkin. "Well, if you dislike him that much, Andy, it's good enough for me. I'm sure he deserves being redistributed."

"He deserves more than that. He left before Rance was born and hasn't contacted Dez or his son until today."

"Which is fine with me." Rance took a gulp of his hot chocolate. "If it wasn't Christmas I'd head off on a little vacay right now. I have no interest in seeing him, talking to him, or listening to his half-assed excuses."

Andy cradled his mug in both hands. "It's probably no comfort, son, but I don't think he's stayed away on account of you. More likely it's because your mom's kicking his butt on the *NYT* list. He's never hit number one and she's done it multiple times. His ego can't handle it."

His body tight with anger, Rance turned toward Desiree. "If that's his issue, and I don't doubt it, why even let him come? Call him back. Say he's not welcome."

She set her mug carefully on the coffee table and held her son's gaze. "He was crying on the phone."

"Who cares?"

"Two months ago he had a heart attack that almost killed him."

"Oh, so now he's afraid he'll go to hell if he dies before making peace with the son he abandoned for almost thirty years?" His voice shook. "And I'm supposed to welcome him with open arms? Forget it, Mom."

Lani fought an instinctive urge to squeeze his arm and communicate her support. But doing that might reveal... too much. Gripping her mug in both hands, she stared at the bits of whipped cream floating on top of the chocolate.

"I'm not saying I believe he's changed, son. I'm not welcoming him with open arms and I haven't even begun to forgive him for his behavior."

"Then call him. Please, Mom. Tell him you've reconsidered."

"But you see, I haven't. This isn't about him. I don't give a damn about him. It's about you."

"And I don't want him here! Please call him and tell him—"

"This is a chance for you to be a bigger man, a better man than he is or ever will be. You don't have to love him. You don't even have to like him. But summoning the courage to meet him face-to-face with civility will give you so much power."

He sucked in a breath and slowly let it out. "What if all I want to do is punch him?"

"You'll just shove your hands in your pockets. You're a McLintock."

"Hey," Andy said, "I'm not a McLintock. Can I punch him?"

Lani chuckled and glanced at Andy. "I'll be glad to hold your drink while you beat the crap out of him."

He winked at her. "Deal."

But she and Andy were only bystanders, not the main players in this drama. Locked in a silent battle of wills, Rance and Desiree stared at each other.

Rance caved first. "Okay." He blew out a breath. "I guess there could be some satisfaction in letting him know I've survived just fine without him."

"Exactly. Survived and thrived."

"Having him show up now is funny, in a way. I can't say whether the timing is the worst in the world or it's perfectly appropriate considering why I'm here this morning."

Lani tensed. The news about Irving Quick's arrival had made her temporarily forget their reason for coming. Granny had mentioned that Desiree's feelings might be hurt because she hadn't been the first to know. Her emotions were already running high. How would she react?

She regarded Rance with outward calm. "They say surprises come in threes. I'm ready for the second one."

Rance took a deep breath. "I've written a book."

17

"Oh, my God! That's fabulous!"

Instantly Rance regretted not giving the manuscript to his mom. He could have given one to her and one to Lani. Hadn't figured that out until now.

His mom scooted forward in the chair as if ready to launch herself at him and Sam dashed over to see what was going on. "I've always hoped you'd decide to write."

"Fiction? Is it fiction?" Andy beamed at him. "I hope so because—"

"It is." He stroked Sam's silky head and fought a queasy sensation in his stomach. "A Western." What was done was done. It had made sense when he was planning this, but—

"A Western! Even better! I can't wait to—"

"It's contemporary and has a mystery in it. It's gonna be a series."

"I'm *so* excited, son." Her eyes glistened. "I knew if any of my kids decided to write, you'd be the likely one, but then you seemed happy bartending. When did you start it?"

"February."

"And you've kept it a secret all this time? Or am I the last to know?"

"I didn't want anyone to find out, but...Lani knows now." He glanced at her for moral support. She gave him a quick smile, which helped. He took another breath and faced his mom. "In fact, she's read it."

"Oh!" Shock and a flash of disappointment registered in her eyes, but she recovered fast. "Well, I can see why you'd... she's an editor after all."

Might as well spill all the beans and get it over with. "I'm submitting it to her publisher."

"You are? I mean, that's your choice, of course, but..." Gradually the confusion in her expression cleared. Her breath hitched. "You want to do this on your own."

"I do, Mom. I know you'd offer me all your resources and I appreciate that more than I can say. But then I'd never really know if I made it because of my book, because of your connections, or simply because I'm your son."

She took a shaky breath and nodded. "I understand. I like to think I'd give it an impartial reading, but maybe not. Do you... do you even want me to read it?"

"Absolutely! We brought two copies, one for you and one for Andy."

"Where are they?"

"In the truck. I was so focused on making it into the house, I forgot to grab the box."

Andy left his chair. "The wind's died down. I think the storm's letting up. I'll go get ''em."

Rance stood. "With all due respect, Andy, you're not fetching that box. If anybody's going out there, it's me."

"Or..." Andy's blue eyes reflected a hint of steel. "We can go out together, get some fresh air and take Sam."

The collie picked right up on that suggestion, nails clicking on the wood floor like castanets.

"It's not *War and Peace* Andy. We don't need both of us to haul in the box."

He just smiled. "I love stepping outside after a snow, don't you? The world looks like it just got a fresh coat of paint."

No percentage in arguing with Andy when he'd set his mind to a task. The guy was tenacious as a honey badger and for some reason he wanted to be part of retrieving those manuscripts. He likely had something to say. "Sure, we can do that."

"Take your time," his mom said. "I'll get the scoop on what Lani thought of the book."

He wasn't crazy about Lani giving her a preview, but that wasn't his call.

"Sorry, Desiree. My lips are sealed. I'm sure Rance wants you to read it with no preconceptions."

Later he'd give her lips a big ol' kiss for that response. "Thanks, Lani." He sent a look of gratitude her way before following Andy and Sam to the front door.

Conversation began immediately once he'd turned his back, but not about him. Sounded like a discussion about the caroling. Good Lord, his worthless father would be here for that. Probably fancied himself a singer. Anger curdled in his gut.

In the entry, Andy toed off his leather boots and put on rubber snow boots. "Your mom's right, you know."

"Yeah, she is." He pulled a spare pair of rubber boots from the closet. "That doesn't mean I have to like the idea of facing that creep."

"Look at it this way. He'll be alone. No allies. You have your whole family standing with you. Sky and Beau are old enough to remember him. They hate his guts." He put on his hooded parka.

"I didn't know that." He smiled. "Good info."

"Clint and Cheyenne were only four so their memory is hazy, which gives them license to make up terrible stories about him because they *could* be true."

"I love it. How come I've never heard any of them?"

"You kept the subject locked down so they decided you didn't want to talk about him."

"I didn't, but it's nice to know they were hating on him behind my back." He finished buttoning his coat and crammed his hat on his head. "Let's do this."

Andy unhooked a towel from the coat rack. "For Sam."

"Good call."

Reaching for the door, Andy pulled it open to reveal a world transformed. A few flakes drifted down from the cloud-covered sky, but the storm was over.

A crust of snow had formed against the bottom of the door. Stepping over it, Andy walked out on the porch, his boots crunching on several inches of the white stuff. Sam streaked past him, scattering snow as he bounded down the steps and leaped through the drifts with yips of joy.

"There goes your fresh paint job." Rance closed the door behind him and stood beside the man who'd been more of a father to him in the past two years than his biological parent ever could be.

Irving Quick had zero chance of gaining parental status. The position belonged to his mom, Andy, Buck and Marybeth, the four people he credited with molding him into a decent human being.

Even some of the other dads had treated him with fatherly affection, bringing gifts and encouraging him in whatever activity he happened to be into when they visited. Gestures like theirs emphasized that his father was, in Andy's words, a dick.

He let out a breath, creating a cloud of condensation. "Thanks for reminding me I have a cheering section."

"I'd say it's a lot more powerful than that." Andy fished gloves out of his coat pocket and put them on. "Quick has no idea what he's getting into. He left a woman surrounded by little kids and a kindly couple who were helping her raise them. The McLintocks have become a force to be reckoned with and he's inflicted harm on one of their own. I don't envy him."

"Do you feel sorry for him?"

"Hell, no." Andy chuckled. "I can't wait to see his scared rabbit expression when he realizes who he's dealing with and what he's up against. I don't want him here, but since I agree with your mother that you should confront him, I'll take pleasure in watching you reduce him to a sniveling shadow of a man."

"I don't know if I can—"

"Of course you can. You're a writer. Use your words."

"Speaking of that, why did you want to help me get the manuscripts?"

"I needed to find out beforehand if you dedicated it to your mother."

"Sure did."

"Good man. Did you by chance put the dedication page in these manuscripts?"

"I did. Probably an amateur move to include it in a submission, but I wanted her to see it was there, ready to go once it was published."

"I don't care if it's an amateur move. It's the right move, and I intend to make sure she opens to that page immediately."

"I hurt her feelings by not giving it to her first. I know she was disappointed, but—"

"It has to be complicated when you want to write and your mom's already a well-known author."

Andy's kind words eased the turmoil in his gut. "Very complicated." Watching Sam cavorting in the snow helped, too.

"At least she doesn't write under her own name. I didn't think to ask. Are you using a pseudonym?"

"I'm not planning to. Rance McLintock sounds like a Western writer. But if I want another layer of anonymity, I could go that route. Her real name is getting out there and it'll be in the dedication."

"It's out there but it doesn't have traction. Not many will make the connection. If you don't draw attention to it, you should be able to use your real name and find your own success independent of hers."

"I hope so. Eventually it won't matter, but with this first book, especially since it's a Western...."

"I totally get it. She does, too. And seeing the dedication will go a long way to soothe her ruffled feathers."

Rance gazed at him. "I didn't realize how much you look out for her."

"Always."

"It's nice, Andy."

"It's nice that she lets me. There was a time she couldn't imagine leaning on anyone."

"Maybe because you're the first solid guy she's come across. Anyway, if that's all you're here for, to find out about the dedication, you might as well stay on the porch while I go fetch the box."

"There was one other thing."

"Oh?"

"I can't help thinking you had an ulterior motive for giving Lani the book."

He grimaced. "I did, but things didn't work out the way I'd hoped. I can't see her leaving that job. You should see her face when she talks about it."

"You should see her face when she looks at you. And vice-versa."

"That obvious, huh?"

'Yes."

"To everyone?"

"Yes."

"I wish I could say it'll all turn out, but I can't see a path leading to a happy-ever-after."

"Gonna keep looking for one?"

"Yes, sir."

"That's my boy. Now go get those manuscripts while I use this towel on Sam."

"Yes, sir." He headed down the snow-covered steps. *That's my boy.* Andy might not know how much those simple words meant. He was Andy's boy and so were his brothers. Angie was his girl as much as Jess, the daughter he'd sired.

Andy hadn't just married their mom. He'd married all of them, stepping into the role of father with grace, compassion and a wicked sense of humor. Who needed effing Irving Quick? He had Andy Hartmann.

_18_

Lani wasn't particularly proud of her singing ability, but she let Desiree talk her into joining the carolers since Sara and Kieran were going.

"You won't have a thing to worry about," Desiree said. "We have strong singers like Kieran, Faye, Gil and Tyra to keep us in tune. Rance has a decent voice. I'll rope him in when he and Andy get back."

"Am I right you've never done this before?"

"We haven't. I got the idea when I realized we'd be renting a flatbed to transport the sleigh into town on Christmas Eve and it would make a perfect hay wagon for caroling. Buck's offered to use his truck to pull us around to all the houses."

"I guess you'll skip Gil and Faye's though, since nobody will be in their cabin." Lani polished off the last of her hot chocolate and returned the mug to the tray.

"Actually, someone will be there. Faye and Ella's folks are staying there from tomorrow night through Christmas, so we'll definitely stop for a song or two."

"They'll be here for Christmas dinner, then. How many does that make? I've lost track."

"It keeps growing. We started with under thirty, not counting kids. We're over that, now, and all three dads want to come."

"Four dads."

Desiree made a face. "Four dads. Unless the animosity gets to him and he leaves early. I wish he hadn't picked Christmas to descend on us. Weird timing. He has a wife and kids."

"Really? He's leaving them to come here?"

"He's determined to make a significant gesture or so he said. He's spent every Christmas with them and no Christmases with his firstborn and he wants to right that wrong."

"Wow. He gets to ruin Christmas for us and them at the same time. That's special."

"I won't let him ruin ours. His family may be delighted to spend Christmas without him, especially since he didn't tell them about Rance until last week."

"You're kidding."

"Nope. Rance was a big dark secret. If I were his wife I'd be ready to strangle him, both for abandoning a child he'd fathered and lying to her and his other two kids all these years."

"No wonder he's coming here for Christmas."

"Well, if he expects a warm welcome he'll be sadly disappointed. Sky and Beau remember him. They didn't like him then and after it became clear he wasn't going to acknowledge, let alone visit Rance, they had no use for him. They've encouraged their siblings to despise him, too."

"What was the appeal? Wait... that's too personal. Sorry. Never mind. I didn't mean to—"

"That's okay. It's not a secret. I'd read one of his books and thought it was pretty good. He had a signing up in Missoula, so I left the kids with Buck and Marybeth and drove up to get my book autographed. We talked for hours. I'd never known another successful writer and it was great fun to find a kindred spirit. One thing led to another."

Lani nodded. "And he's good-looking."

"Yeah, I was a sucker for that smile. Rance has it."

"I suppose he does, now that you mention it." Her act likely wasn't fooling Desiree, but she'd keep it up for now. "How long were you together?"

"A couple of months. My first mistake was making the *New York Times* list while he was here. He claimed it was all rigged, had nothing to do with popularity, blah, blah, blah. Then he started criticizing my work."

"Charming."

"I was ready to send him packing, but I hadn't decided when and how. Then I discovered I was pregnant. I gave him the news and he couldn't leave fast enough. His call this morning was the first contact he's made since he walked out the door."

"He was only here for two months and yet Sky and Beau remember him?"

"Oh, yeah. Clint and Cheyenne say they do, too, but they were only four, so they could be piggybacking on what Sky and Beau remember."

"Was he mean to them?"

"I wouldn't have stood for that. He was outwardly kind, but all the kids took a dislike to him right away, which I should have seen as a bad sign. Kids sense when somebody's not genuine. Buck and Marybeth didn't care for him, either, but I didn't find that out until the day he left. We had a party to celebrate. We had cake, ice cream, the works."

Lani chuckled. "I can see how that stuck in their minds. Cake and ice cream make things memorable when you're a kid."

"I also think that's why everyone loved Angie's dad Gene so much. He came along after I had Rance and adopted Lucky. Gene was the flip side of Irv. Sky and Beau pointed it out constantly. *Mommy, Gene fixed my bike! Irv couldn't do that. Gene taught us to whistle! Bet Irv doesn't even know how.*"

"It's sad that he died."

"It was awful. But I wouldn't change anything. Because of Irv I have Rance and Lucky. In the final analysis, I ended up with the best of the best." She glanced toward the entry as the door opened. "Does that man know his cue or what?" She winked at Lani. "Hey, you guys! We were about to notify Search and Rescue!"

"We decided to give Sam plenty of time to enjoy the snow," Andy called back. "And before you ask, he's been dried off. He was a good boy so I'm getting him a treat."

"Thanks, my love."

Moments later, Rance walked in, cheeks ruddy, either from the cold or excitement or both. Sam trotted after him, a dog biscuit in his teeth, and headed for his dog bed near the fire. Andy followed and took his customary seat to the left of the sofa.

"Ta-da!" Rance stepped over to the coffee table and set down a slightly bigger box than the one he'd given her. Opening it, he took out the top manuscript. "Presenting *Tequila Shots in the Dark* by Rance McLintock."

Desiree clapped her hands together. "Great title! You're using your own name?"

"Yes, ma'am. I've always liked it and it fits the genre." He handed it over and took out the other one. "Andy, here's yours."

"Can't wait. Looks like a good length — not too long and not too short."

Lani couldn't be sure, but Desiree's copy looked crisper than Andy's. He'd likely given Andy the one she'd read, which was slightly dented up, even though she'd tried to be careful with it.

Desiree held hers on her lap and smoothed her hand over the title page, almost caressing it.

Would she turn to the next page? Lani couldn't wait for her reaction to Rance's heartfelt dedication. She'd been moved by it. Guaranteed Desiree would be over the moon.

"Your first book." Desiree seemed content to leave the manuscript unopened. "I remember when I finished my first one. It's like giving birth — a hell of a lot of work, but oh, the feeling when you've finished." She glanced up. "You're proud of it. I can tell."

He stood with his hands in his pockets and a little-boy grin on his face. "Yeah."

Andy reached for his glasses lying on a side table. "It really is a catchy title. I hope you get to keep it."

"I hope so, but Lani's boss may want something different." He glanced at her.

"It's hard to say. I like it, but in the end it's a marketing decision." Should she tell Desiree to turn the page? No. This wasn't her deal.

Desiree sighed. "Marketing is such a mixed bag. Sometimes my publisher's marketing department gets it right, but they also can get it wrong. I have more say than I used to, but lately I've been thinking about publishing the books myself."

"Seriously?" Rance's eyebrows shot up. "After all this time?"

"A lot of authors are doing it these days."

"What about getting books into the stores?"

"I'd have to handle it, or better yet hire someone to handle it. I have the resources to do that now. Plus I'd take home more of the profits."

"True."

"And if I don't end up in every single venue, that's okay. I've had my day of seeing my books in the airport. I'm over it. But when I started out, I wanted to be in every bookstore in the country and I needed a publisher to make that happen."

"And you're everywhere. That's why I want to keep our relationship on the downlow. I don't want anyone tipping off the *New York Times.*"

"I'll keep my mouth shut. Is that one of your reasons for choosing Lani's publishing house? Less chance of a leak?"

"Yes. Assuming they choose me. I can't take that for granted."

Desiree gazed at him. "Humility becomes you, son. Keep that attitude and you'll be okay, no matter how famous you get."

"You think I'll be famous? Even before you've read the book?"

"I've always thought you'd be famous."

"You never told me that."

She grinned. "If I'd told you any sooner than today, when you've laid your heart and soul on the chopping block, you would have been insufferable."

Lani hid a smile. Desiree knew her son and clearly loved him, warts and all.

"Hey, Dez," Andy said. "You might want to look on the second page."

Finally.

Desiree flipped the title page aside. "What's… oh. Oh, my." She fumbled in the pocket of her jeans and pulled out a tissue. "Oh, Rance. That's… damn. I'm gonna blubber."

"That's the idea." He crouched next to her chair. "You're my inspiration, always have been. You lit the path." His voice grew husky. "I owe you everything."

"I got… I got tear stains… on the page."

He put an arm around her shoulders. "Happy tears."

"Uh-huh. So h-happy."

Lani's throat tightened. She glanced over at Andy, who'd taken off his glasses to wipe his eyes with a bandana.

Tucking the bandana in his hip pocket, he gave her a soft smile. "Good stuff."

"The best." Such wonderful people. No matter what the future held for her and Rance, this moment would stay with her forever.

19

Rance gave his mom a big hug and stood. "I should probably check with Clint about whether he's opening the Buffalo at eleven this morning. If so, I need to take Lani back home so I can give myself plenty of time to drive that two-lane."

"I know what I'll be doing for most of the day," his mom said. "I'll be reading your book."

"That makes two of us." Andy stood. "Time to build up this fire and get cozy."

And now Rance had himself a problem. His foolproof excuse for spending time with Lani tonight had a fatal flaw. If he told his mom and Andy that Lani had suggestions for improving the manuscript, they'd be looking for flaws instead of reading for pleasure.

Andy might be able to ignore that information as he read. But his mother wouldn't be able to. She'd dive into the story with one goal — to find the issues that Lani had identified. Her reading experience would be completely altered.

He needed another excuse and he needed it fast. Tonight had become more critical than ever now that his worthless father would be in town tomorrow.

"I'm finally putting all this together." His mom tapped the manuscript. "This was the manuscript you took over to Rance's last night to get Granny's opinion on some Irish dialogue."

"It was." Lani glanced up at him. "How much should I say?"

"I don't think we're giving anything away by admitting the book has Irish dialogue and you wanted to have Granny confirm that it was accurate."

His mom laughed. "Great minds, son. I'm putting an Irish character in my next book. Listening to Granny inspired me, too."

"That'll be fun, seeing how each of us handled it." Okay, he had a potential plan. "Oh, and Granny made her famous Irish pound cake for dessert last night, and Lani fell in love with it."

Andy adjusted the fireplace screen on the hearth. "She does a good job with that."

"Anyway, Lani's coming over again tonight so Granny can show her how to make it." He flashed her a smile and said a little prayer that she'd go along with his off-the-cuff brainstorm.

Her eyelids quivered for a nanosecond and then she was off and running. "I am. Our family's big on homemade Christmas gifts, so this'll be the perfect thing to give my folks." She avoided looking at him, though.

"I'm a fan of homemade gifts, myself." Andy returned to his seat. "A homemade gift is what brought Dez and me together."

"Oh, yeah?" Lani turned to him. "Who made the gift, you or her?"

"We made it together. We built a playhouse for Maverick."

"What fun!"

"It was that." His mom sent Andy a fond glance. "But I confess I didn't know what I was getting into."

He grinned. "With the project or me?"

"Both, but at least with you I didn't need instructions. What you see is what you get."

"That's Andy, all right." Rance loved that about the guy. The same couldn't be said of him. He'd always been a shapeshifter, a secret-keeper.

He'd planned to send a group text about his book, not because he couldn't wait to tell his siblings, but because it was part of an elaborate plan to buy time with Lani. He'd been forced to use pound cake production instead.

Subterfuge came easily to him, maybe too easily. He justified the current scheme as protecting Lani. She didn't want her folks to know they were getting chummy.

But intrigue was in his DNA, and he took pride in exercising his talent for it. That said, did he want to stage a big reveal about the book on Christmas Day like he'd originally envisioned?

Nope. Most likely Irving Quick would be there poisoning the air he breathed. He pulled out his phone. "Just so you know, you don't have to keep the book a secret." He started composing a message. "I'm writing a group text."

"Hang on a sec," his mom said. "Wouldn't it be more fun to save it for Christmas Day? We can keep it under wraps until then."

"We sure can, son. Seems like the kind of thing you'd want to tell them in person."

"I'd planned to, but..."

Andy swore softly. "It's Quick-dick, isn't it?"

"Yeah. Have you sent out the word about him, Mom?"

"No. I had to tell you first. And I agree the timing sucks."

"When's he getting into town?"

"Probably around eleven, depending on traffic."

"Fortunately I'll be at work."

"Probably just as well. Anyway, I hate to say it, but you shouldn't announce this on Christmas Day, after all. I didn't think of Irv when I suggested it. I don't trust him to be kind and I definitely don't trust him to keep the news to himself."

"Then I'll send the text and tell them it's to stay in the family for now."

"Or you could make the announcement on New Year's Eve," Lani said. "Surely he'll be gone by then."

"God, I hope so." He looked up from his phone and glanced at her. "But I don't want to wait that long."

"Are my folks on that group text?"

"They are. Don't you want them to know?"

"I absolutely want them to know. I just wasn't sure you thought of them as...."

"Family?"

"Yeah. I mean, Dallas has been around a while, but the rest of us only showed up less than a year ago."

He looked over at his mother. "Want to take this?"

"Nah, you go ahead."

He turned back to Lani. "Time's not a factor. Lucky became family in minutes when Mom brought him home from the hospital along with me. When Angie chose Dallas, all the Armstrongs instantly became family. That's how we do things." He smiled. "Whether you like it or not."

"I like it."

"Good to know." He held her gaze too long. He realized it when Andy chuckled. Returning his attention to his phone, he finished the group message and hit Send. Then he excused himself and walked into the library to call Clint.

His big brother answered on the first ring. "Hey, you beat me to it, bro! Congratulations! Way to fly under the radar. Been keeping a laptop under the bar?"

"I promise I didn't write while I was on duty. That wouldn't be fair to you and Tyra."

"Then when did you write it?"

"Before work. After work. Whenever I got some extra time."

"Since when?"

"February."

"That's impressive. While I've been dinking around with our kitchen cabinet remodel, you wrote a whole book. I want to hear all about it when you come in today."

"That's why I called. I—uh-oh. That's Lucky trying to get me. I didn't think about what would happen when I sent that text."

"Your phone's gonna be ringing all day. Wish I could give you the time off, but I need you here."

"You're already at the Buffalo?"

"Yessir. Tyra and I came in early to prep for Christmas Eve. Lots to do before then. We wondered if we'd get snowed in, but the plows are out, both in town and on the two-lane. You should be able to make it, no problem."

"Then I'll see you soon." He disconnected and called Lucky back.

Lucky didn't bother with a greeting. "You wrote a whole damn book and didn't tell me until it was finished? What the hell? Did you tell anybody, because if you told anybody and didn't tell me, I'm gonna—"

"Granny. I told Granny. I had to since she was living with me. I didn't let her read it except the parts with Irish dialogue."

"Okay, Granny, then. I get that, but bro! You had to be writing it for a while, months, if not years. I can't believe you didn't tell me."

"I've been writing since February. You of all people should know why I didn't tell anybody. Oksana kept hers a secret even after it was finished. She'd already started the second book before she told you."

His brother exhaled. "Yeah, but she'd only known me for something like a year. You, on the other hand... we're... dammit, you could've trusted me with this."

The hurt in Lucky's voice hit him hard. "I'm sorry. The truth is, I was scared shitless. I didn't trust myself... to keep going, to follow through. I didn't know with absolute certainty I'd finish it until I did. Even then I kept tweaking it, looking for weak points, rewriting dialogue to make it snappier."

"What made you call it good and announce it to the family?"

"When Lani read it and didn't puke."

"You gave it to *Lani*? When I could've—"

"I decided my first reader should be someone who didn't love me, someone who would tell me the unvarnished truth."

"I would've done that! Mom would've—"

"Would you? Would she? C'mon, bro. You would have sugarcoated it."

"Would not."

"Would so. Admit it. You worship the ground I walk on."

"Not anymore. Damned turncoat." But his muttered words had lost their bite.

"By the way, I did just give it to Mom about fifteen minutes ago. And I told her I was submitting to a small publishing house, specifically Lani's, because I want to do this on my own, not through her, her agent or her publisher. I need to know—"

"All right, all right." He heaved a sigh. "I'm starting to see the method to your madness. Mom and I might be slightly prejudiced."

"You think?"

"And there is a difference between Mom helping Oksana move up the ladder and anointing you as the prodigal son."

"Big difference. Oksana's not writing Westerns. I am. I could easily piggyback on Mom's career. That wouldn't work for me. And... and now Angie just popped up on my screen. Shoulda known she'd be next. I'll call her back."

"Who were you talking to when I called?"

"Clint, to find out if the Buffalo's open today."

"Is it?"

"Yep. The roads are gonna be clear and I need to get going."

"Then the four of us will see you in town."

"The four of you?"

"Kieran and Sara are over here helping Oksana and me decorate our tree."

"Right. I knew that."

"We were gonna hang out here, but I see a trip to the Buffalo in our future. I'm not through chewing your ass, and the other three have a ton of questions."

"I can't stand around gabbing. We'll be busy."

"We'll chose our moments carefully. By the way, when do I get my copy?"

"As soon as I have a chance to print more."

"You'll need a bunch and chances are you'll run out of time, ink and paper."

"Thanks for the vote of confidence, bro."

"Ah, but I have a solution. Bring a copy with you, give it to me when we get there, and we'll hop over to the shop and make copies while you're bartending. My printer's better and faster."

Rance laughed. "You're getting ballsy in your old age."

"Damn straight, and it's your fault. Yours and Oksana's."

"That makes me proud. I'll take a copy to work. See you soon." He disconnected and checked the time. Calling Angie back would likely make him late for work. And after promising Lucky a copy of the book, he'd have to ask Granny for hers, after all.

Lucky had quickly figured out everyone would want copies. But printing out that many would be asking a lot. He'd suggest to Lucky that one copy per couple was enough. His phone lit up again. Beau.

Somehow he'd failed to consider that his group text would create a tsunami of phone calls. He let Beau's go to voice mail and sent another group text apologizing for getting everyone riled up when he had to leave for work and couldn't respond.

Lani came to the door of the library. "We should go or you'll be—"

"I know. Let's do it." He turned off his phone and tucked it in his pocket, "Mom, Andy, we're leaving!" He started toward the entry.

"See you later," his mother called back. "Drive safely."

"I will!"

Lani kept pace with him. "You look stressed."

"I didn't plan this very well. I didn't anticipate that the text would create so much excitement."

"Didn't you?" She shoved her feet into her boots.

"I know, I know. I should have, but I didn't, and now everybody wants to talk to me. Or in Lucky's case, give me hell for not telling him sooner." He helped her on with her coat and shrugged into his own.

"Lucky's upset?"

"He was. I think he's okay now. But stirring up my sibs might give us a logistical problem." He tugged on the brim of his hat, opened the door and ushered her out. The snow on the porch was already starting to melt.

"They'll want to get together?"

"They might, especially after Mom sends her text about Irving Quick." He took her hand as they started down the steps but released it at the bottom. "Just follow the path I made when I fetched the manuscripts. While I was at it I created one around to the passenger side."

"Good thinking."

"On that subject, at least. On others I'm not doing so hot." He followed her to the truck while mulling over the complications he'd added to what used to be a sweet little scheme.

While she walked around the tailgate, he climbed behind the wheel, started the engine and cranked up the heat. She wasted no time hopping in and buckling up. He shifted into reverse and Thunder did the rest, digging through the snow until they were headed back out the way they'd come.

Lani glanced at him. "Sounds like our plans might have to change."

"They might, except no matter what, I've obligated you to make a pound cake."

"Fine with me. When did you figure out that we couldn't use the other excuse?"

"Late in the game, I'm ashamed to say. Not until I handed over the manuscripts and mom said she'd spend the day reading."

"I realized it when she wanted me to give her the scoop on your book while you guys were outside. It would have been the perfect time to mention I had suggestions. And by doing that I'd taint her reading experience, even if I didn't tell her what they were."

"You were way ahead of me on that score. Thanks for jumping on board with the pound cake idea."

"I thought it was ingenious, assuming Granny wants to."

"I'm pretty sure she will. She keeps trying to get me to make one, but much as I love her, I don't wanna. I hope you're at least mildly interested."

"I'm totally interested. I wasn't kidding about giving it to my folks. They can buy whatever they want which makes finding the right gift a challenge."

"Glad to hear it's not a lame idea." He took a steadying breath. "And I'll figure out a way we can spend some time together tonight, no matter what."

"Hey, this is your big moment. Your family wants to be with you and celebrate this achievement. Seems to me that should be the priority."

"Logically, you're right." He glanced at her. "But I'm on fire, Lani-lou. Burning like I've never burned before. Logic doesn't stand a chance."

20

The heat in Rance's eyes made Lani squirm in her seat. If only he could pull over and do something about it. Wishful thinking. He had to go to work and she'd have questions from her folks the minute she walked through the door.

Or not. As her parents' turnoff came into view, their yellow truck pulled onto the main ranch road.

Rance beeped a greeting and her dad did the same. Her mom gave a wave.

"Looks like you'll have the house to yourself."

"It does. I'm not sure where they're going. They didn't have any specific plans for today."

"Wish I could stay and steal a few kisses."

"It would be more than a few and you know it."

"Yeah, it would." He made the turn. "Just as well I can't stay. We don't know where they're going or when they'll be back."

Lani's phone chimed. "We're about to find out." She quickly read the text from her mom. "They offer their congrats on the book. They're heading to the barn so Buck can give them lessons in driving the sleigh. They want to take a turn on Christmas Eve."

"Yeah? That's awesome."

"After that they're going into town to meet with the committee for the event. The chair called this morning."

"There's a committee?"

"Evidently."

"Clearly the idea's taken on a life of its own. Shows you how little attention I've paid to anything but the book. That's cool, though, about your folks getting involved."

"I'm not surprised. It's their kind of thing."

"And I'm really sad I can't stay." He pulled up to her folks' cabin. "Listen, I don't think this pound cake idea will work the way I hoped. Between my book and Irving Quick, the gang will want to have a potluck tonight at Rowdy Roost. I can feel it coming."

"Then no dinner at your house?"

"I doubt it. That doesn't mean we won't eventually have time alone. I'm determined to find a way. But you still need a pound cake." He got out his phone. "What if I call and see if she'd have time now?"

"Okay, but I'd have no way to get... oh, wait. Kieran and Sara are at Lucky's. That might work, depending on timing."

"If not, someone else can run you home. I can check with—"

"You know what? Don't worry about it. If Granny doesn't mind having me around, I'm happy to spend the day with her. Go ahead and call."

He turned on his phone, which greeted him with a rapid set of pings.

She blinked. "Texts?"

"And even more voicemails. I turned it off so we could drive over here in peace." He tapped the screen and waited as Granny's phone rang. "That's weird. Why isn't she answering?"

"In the shower?"

"She likes to shower before dinner." When the voicemail came on, he frowned and disconnected. "No point in leaving a message. She won't find it." He tapped the phone again. Still no answer. "We're outta here." Throwing the truck in reverse, he backed quickly around and hit the gas going down the lane to the ranch road.

He drove even faster once he made the turn, spraying snow, his jaw set. With his attention glued to the road ahead, he quietly unbuckled his seat belt.

Her gut clenched. "I'm sure she's fine." She wasn't sure at all. It was a dumb thing to say, but she couldn't come up with anything better. Granny was *fine*. She'd been in great shape last night at dinner, right?

Of course she'd worked all day on that dinner. She'd excused herself early, which Lani had taken as part of the scheme. What if she'd pushed too hard making that dinner? What if—

Rance skidded on the turn onto his road, came out of it quickly and shot forward. Slamming on the brakes when they reached the cabin, he rammed the gearshift into park and flung open his door. "Sit still. Let me see—"

"The hell with that!" She unbuckled and scrambled out.

He was already on the porch, calling for Granny as he wrenched open the front door and barreled inside.

Lani charged after him. Did he know CPR? If not, could she do it? She'd taken a class once, but she hadn't practiced. What were the steps?

Racing past the open door, she found Rance smothering Granny in a hug and rocking back and forth while they both laughed. He was swearing and Granny's *feck, feck, feck* likely qualified as swearing in Ireland.

She was okay. Lani's breath whooshed out. Thank God. Rance's manuscript lay upside down on the floor, pages splayed out. Obviously Granny had been reading it. Had she been so engrossed she hadn't heard the phone?

Peeking out from Rance's tight embrace, Granny spotted her. "Oh, luv, tis scarlet I am, scarin' ya so! Now if ya will excuse me, I'll go put in m'ears."

Oh. Lani swallowed a laugh as she met Rance's long-suffering gaze. "Well, if we needed any more proof that she's deaf...."

"I did not. And I just aged at least ten years. See any gray in my hair? I'll bet I have gray hairs, now."

"Tis back I am." Granny bustled in, all smiles.

Rance turned to her. "We need to make some rules."

"Ya want me to wear my hearin' aids when yer out and about?"

"Yes, please."

"I didna expect ya to call."

"I didn't expect to call, either, but I thought you put your hearing aids in first thing in the morning."

"That I do, so I can hear what yer sayin', but when ya leave, I take 'em out again."

"I didn't know that." His chest heaved. "I haven't been that scared in... forever."

She reached over and patted his cheek. "Yer a good boy, Rance McLintock, rushin' to find out if I'm dead."

"I didn't think you were—"

"Yeah, ya did. Yer face was white as a polar bear's ass. So what were ya callin' me for?"

"To ask a favor for me," Lani said. "Since my folks adore your pound cake, I'd like to make them one as a Christmas present, if you'd be willing to teach me how. And if you have time."

"That's brilliant!" She clapped her hands together. "When?"

"Now? I hate to interrupt your reading, though."

"Oh! Rance's book!" She glanced at the floor. "Where did—"

"Right here." He held it up. "I have a favor to ask, too. Can I borrow this for the day? In fact, I can bring you a fresh copy. This one's kinda dinged up."

"Threw it in the air, I did. Thought an avalanche was bearin' down on us."

He smiled. "We're too far from the mountains to be hit by an avalanche."

"Now ya tell me. After I memorized all the ways ta survive one. Anyway, sure, take it. Lani needs me ta help her make a pound cake."

"In that case, I'll shove off."

"Are you workin' till five, again, lad?"

"I am, but I'll find someone to come and fetch Lani whenever you two are finished."

Granny looked at her. "Are ya in a hurry to go somewhere, luv?"

"No, but I don't want to impose."

"Ya wouldn't. We'll have a grand time gettin' ta know each other better. Take off yer coat. Make yerself at home."

"Thank you." She hung it on the rack by the door while Rance and Granny held a murmured conversation. She turned back in time to catch Granny standing on tiptoe to give him a kiss on the cheek. So cute.

Then she made a shooing motion. "Go on with ya, boy, before ya make yerself late."

"Thanks, Granny. Oh, and get Lani to tell you the latest news. Better her than me. She can probably do it without swearing." Tipping his hat, he headed out the door clutching his manuscript.

He must have found a source in town for printing more of them. Probably Lucky, who'd have a printer at his shop and then he'd be the first of the siblings to get a copy.

Excitement was building throughout the family. That had to feel good, despite his frustration about the rendezvous that might never happen.

"Ya fancy him."

"Pretty obvious, huh?"

"Like yer wearin' one of those sandwich boards. Do yer mum and dad know?"

"I haven't told them, but...."

"Yeah, they know. Like I said, it's stickin' out all over ya."

She laughed. "I've got Rance fever."

"There's worse things, luv. He's a fine lad."

"Yes, he is. But I know myself. If I left Square Glasses Press to move out here, there's no comparable job for me. Eventually I'd become resentful."

"Know somethin' about that, I do. When my Fiona left for America, I was teachin' school. Loved it. I quit ta care for little Kieran. By the time I could've gone back, everythin' had changed and m'heart wasn't in it. I held it against Fiona for years."

"I'll bet you were a great teacher."

Her face lit up. "There were those that said so." She motioned toward the kitchen. "Let's get started. Ya can see for yerself. Got a spare apron, I do."

Lani had never worn an apron in her life, but she put on the flowered one Granny offered her.

That competent lady had clearly taken charge of Rance's kitchen. She moved around it with authority, assembling ingredients. "Rance thinks we'll all be at a gatherin' tonight. He said so before he left."

"I think so, too. That's why he wants to get copies made, so he can pass them out."

"But yer plan's banjaxed." Taking two sticks of butter from the fridge, she laid them on the counter. "We hafta let these warm up. Eggs, too."

"What's banjaxed?"

She pulled out a carton of eggs and put six in a bowl. "Ya know, when everythin' goes to shit."

Lani snorted. "Then we're banjaxed."

Turning around, Granny gave her a bright-eyed glance. "Any ideas?"

"Not yet."

"Then we'll hafta come up with some, won't we, now?"

"You and me?"

"Why not? I told him we would. That boy's too busy and we've got all day."

21

What a day. Rance drove home at a leisurely pace for a change, using the half-hour to decompress. The Buffalo had been wall-to-wall customers from the moment the doors opened. Most of them had wanted a table and ordered something to eat.

Not his family. They'd arrived intermittently throughout the afternoon just to order a drink at the bar. He hadn't had much time to answer questions, but evidently they'd wanted a chance to study him like some recently discovered lifeform.

They weren't surprised he'd written a book. They'd said as much. But his dogged determination and absolute secrecy while he'd labored over that project for months had blown their minds.

For years he'd been their court jester, patterning himself after Beau and then expanding on the concept. Everyone had thought they knew what made him tick. Clearly they hadn't expected this — a disciplined solo effort that had produced something of value.

To be honest, he'd surprised himself. He hadn't been convinced he could stick with a project for that long without feedback. But the process had taken hold of him and become the most satisfying endeavor he'd ever known.

It had changed him, and clearly it had changed the way his family looked at him. The emotion shining in their eyes made his chest swell and his chin lift. At long last, they respected him.

And wow, were they itching to get their hands on his book. He'd made a deal with Lucky. In exchange for printing more copies, Lucky had taken the first one for himself.

The others were stacked on Thunder's backseat for distribution tonight. Couples would have to share, with copies going to his siblings, plus Trent and Sara.

Buck and Marybeth would get a copy and so would Harry and Vanessa. The Wenches, except for Jess and his mom, would each get one. He had a replacement for the one Granny had tossed in the air. And since Lani had donated hers to the cause, she needed another one, too.

Had he forgotten anybody? He didn't think so, but he could print out more if necessary. Lucky had handled the bulk of it, and with a glad heart, too. Once he'd gotten over the shock of not being in the know, he'd accepted the wisdom of Rance's decisions regarding his first book.

The rush of support from his family had blunted his anger about his father's arrival, a nice bonus. Like Andy had said, Irving Quick had nobody on his side. Rance had a small army.

Now if only he'd dreamed up some way he and Lani could sneak away and be together tonight, even if it was only for a few hours. He was excited about the party at Rowdy Roost but couldn't find a plausible excuse for taking Lani home with him.

Granny had said she'd work on it, or rather she and Lani would work on it. The image of those two plotting a tryst made him smile.

His cherubic-looking octogenarian roommate was a natural. She might be more devious than he was. Not Lani, though, and that was fine. Preferable, even. Except for this circumstance.

Maybe a day spent with Granny might bring out her wily side. He could only hope, because he had zip.

As he made the turn onto his property, happiness flooded his system. Lights from the thirty-footer shone through the trees and soon the lights on his front porch greeted him, along with the glow from the windows.

Until Granny's arrival, he'd always come home to an empty cabin. Tonight that cabin held two people who made his heart sing. His head knew that was a temporary situation but his heart wouldn't listen.

The faint sound of laughter penetrated the cabin walls as he climbed the steps, two manuscripts in his hands. He wasn't surprised that people he loved would enjoy each other. But the evidence warmed him inside and out.

He opened the door to the delicious aroma of baked pound cake and the cheerful sight of both ladies engrossed in a game of pool. He laid the manuscripts on the small table by the door.

Granny gave him a thumbs up but Lani remained focused, sighting down the length of the cue with a muttered *be with you in a minute.*

He understood. Once you were lined up, you needed to hold that position and take the shot. Hooking his Stetson on the rack next to the table, he hung up his coat and hat and started toward the hallway.

Granny let out a gasp. "Jaysus! Are ya bleedin, boyo?"

Lani's head snapped up and her eyes widened in alarm. "Rance! What—"

"It's grenadine. Clint and I were tearing around trying to fill orders and bumped into each other. This happened. I have to change, but then I'll be ready to go if you two are."

"We were just waiting for you." Lani's gaze sparkled with awareness, the pool shot evidently forgotten. "That stuff looks sticky. Did it soak through?"

"Some. I'll need to wash up a bit. Then I'll be ready to go." Innocent conversation. Loaded with innuendo. She wanted to help him with that task. He could see it in her eyes. And Lord, did he want her to. Forcing himself to look away, he started toward the hallway. "Those manuscripts on the table are for you two."

"Thanks, lad," Granny called after him. "Rinse out yer shirt. Might stain if ya don't."

"I'll leave it to soak." He lengthened his stride, escaping the heat before it engulfed him. One searing glance from Lani and he was ready to rumble. How in hell would he make it through this party without dragging her into one of the bedrooms only steps from Rowdy Roost?

He sponged off his chest, filled his bathroom sink with water and left the shirt in it. A peek in the mirror confirmed that he had five o'clock shadow going on, but shaving would hold up the program and he might not be kissing Lani, anyway. What a depressing thought.

Pulling out his favorite green plaid shirt, he put it on and quickly buttoned it. Would Lani be the one unfastening those buttons? The image threatened to give him a woody.

Deep breath. Think of how eager your family is to toast your accomplishment and offer support for the impending arrival of Irving Quick.

He didn't want to think about his damned father, but it did a great job of cooling his jets. Tucking in his shirt, he buckled his belt, ran a comb through his hair and walked into the living room. "Let's do this."

Granny smiled. "Ya wore m'favorite."

"Mine, too." He glanced at the table. The manuscripts were gone. Lani held hers and the other had disappeared, probably into Granny's bedroom. "Did you have time to finish the game?" Everything was back in place, cues in the rack, balls in the pockets.

"We weren't actually playing," Lani said. "Granny was giving me some pointers. I like pool but I still have a lot to learn."

"You can come practice anytime." She was welcome to his pool table, his cabin, his bed, his body — whatever took her fancy.

"Thanks. We'll see how it goes."

Perfect opening. "Did you two come up with any ideas for... tonight?"

"Nothin' grand, that's fer sure," Granny said.

"Semi-grand?"

"Not really." Lani shrugged. "They all depend on things we can't control. How about you?"

He shook his head. "Strategy is supposed to be my superpower, but I'm tapped out. Unless I just announce you're coming home with me...." He checked Lani's expression. Not encouraging.

"Then my family would get their hopes up."

"Yeah, that would be a problem."

"Discussing changes in the manuscript is still the best excuse, but timing is everything. I'll have to call on my skills from drama class. They're rusty."

"Didn't know you were in drama."

"The fantasy of it appeals to me. It's why I love editing fiction. And I'm much better at editing than acting. No promises."

"Understood." But she'd given him a sliver of hope. "I'll think positive."

"I'll light a candle fer ya in my mind."

Lani smiled. "I like that. Anyway, we should probably go." She walked over to the coat rack, put down the manuscript and grabbed her coat. "Thanks for bringing us copies. Are there more?"

"In Thunder's backseat. Lucky printed them." He followed, taking down Granny's coat and holding it while she slid her arms in. "What about the pound cake? Is that going with us?"

"We made two, one for my folks and one for Granny to give Desiree and Andy. I'm leaving mine here until Christmas Eve since there's no way I could smuggle it into the house. Too fragrant."

"True. The house smells great." He tucked Granny into the sturdy wool coat she'd brought from Ireland, the one she'd had more than forty years.

"Wrapped them up real pretty, we did, first in foil and then in some of that horse and sleigh paper." She took a wool hat out of her pocket and pulled it over her blonde curls.

"And they're topped with Granny's bows. She could give a class in how to make beautiful bows. I practiced making a few, but mostly we worked on my pool game. That's what I told my folks I was over here for."

"Good thinking. I wondered if you'd have to explain why you were here all afternoon."

"You know, they're so excited about this sleigh ride committee I don't think they paid much attention."

"And we had a grand time, we did. Also, I got the whole story about the plonker who calls himself yer father. Feel like smackin' him upside the head, I do. Now where's that other mitten?"

He scooped it off the floor. "Here you go." Granny wore mittens, another thing that charmed him.

"Thank ya kindly. I should hook 'em together on a string like I did for Kieran when he was a wee lad."

"You don't need a string. You've got me." Over the top of Granny's head he caught Lani's eye and she smiled. Clearly she was as taken by this adorable woman as he was. "And we're off." He opened the door and ushered them out.

As if by prior agreement, he and Lani each took a side and escorted Granny down the icy steps.

"Just so ya know, I'm sittin' in the backseat."

"Absolutely not." Lani's tone left no room for argument.

But she'd never argued with Granny. He had, and he hadn't won yet. This should be interesting.

"Ya need ta respect yer elders, Lani."

He swallowed a laugh. *Here we go.*

"I do respect my elders," Lani said sweetly. "That's why you should ride in the front."

"But I want ta ride in the back. Ya need ta respect my wishes, luv."

"You can't see as well back there. Please ride in the front. It would make me happy."

"But ya need ta think about what would make *me* happy."

"Of course, but—"

"What would make me happy is ridin' in the back with those manuscripts while yer perched up there next to Rance. Which side are those books on, lad?"

"Behind my seat."

"Perfect. Case closed. If ya could help me in, I'd be obliged."

"Be glad to." He got Granny situated, closed the door and turned back to Lani. "Ready to get in front? Or do you want to ride in the back with Granny and hold the manuscripts on your lap?"

"What just happened?"

He grinned. "You lost your first argument with the most stubborn lady on the planet."

"Why didn't you back me up? She would have listened to you."

"Not once she was dug in. I would've had to throw her over my shoulder and stuff her in the front seat. Which I will never do unless a grizzly is hot on her trail."

"Why is she so adamant?"

"She wants to see us sitting up there, side-by-side."

"That's obvious, but I don't get it. She knows why we won't be a couple. She understands."

"Doesn't mean she's giving up."

"What about you?"

"Not while there's life in my body."

22

Lani's heart was still hammering when Rance climbed behind the wheel and started Thunder's powerful engine. *Not while there's life in my body.*

The intensity in his voice and the heat in his eyes had left her shaking. Good thing he'd helped her into his truck because she wouldn't have made it on her own.

His delivery had stunned her, but so had his words. He was good with them. And good with his hands. And his mouth.

When he'd strolled into the cabin and announced he'd have to strip down and clean up, she'd had to abandon her pool practice. The image of him rubbing a warm washcloth over his manly chest had dampened her panties .

Granny had teased her about her besotted stare. Then she'd urged her to try extra hard to find an excuse to come back here after the party. Oh, she would, even when spending more hours in Rance's arms was a very dumb move on her part.

Dangerous, too. He was potent enough to make her question her decision to keep the job and lose the man. Maybe she could copyedit for the *Sentinel* or become one of Sara's tour guides.

L'Amour and More would have been another possibility, except Lucky didn't need her. He'd just hired two of the Wenches, Annette and Colleen, to work fulltime.

Just as well, because a bookstore would only make her homesick for the world of publishing and that was her passion. The process fascinated her and the staff of Square Glasses Press inspired her. No job in Wagon Train would even come close.

Rance pulled Thunder into a parking spot next to her folks bright yellow F-250. The area resembled the local dealership's truck lot. A year ago she wouldn't have been able to tell a Ford from any of the other brands. Now she could pick them out every time.

Desiree's love of Christmas had turned the ranch house into a fairyland. Although she had sparkling lights in the trees year-round, she doubled the number for the holidays. She'd even hung oversized ornaments from the bare branches of trees closest to the house.

At Granny's suggestion, Rance divided the stack of manuscripts into thirds so each of them could participate in bringing in his precious gift to his family. Someone had shoveled a wide path from the parking area to the porch, where evergreen garlands, lights and bows covered the railing.

A ginormous wreath hung in splendor on the heavy wooden door. She and Rance tag-teamed once again, taking hold of Granny on the way up the steps.

After spending the day with her, Lani believed she could have made it up on her own, but Rance would never forgive himself if she fell. His dedication to her welfare was appealing, too damned appealing.

Andy opened the door before they could use the horseshoe knocker. Every cabin had one, now, all created by Gil and Bret's metalworks shop.

Tucking his phone away, Andy grabbed Sam's collar before the collie could bolt outside. "I'm the official greeter. Sam's my assistant."

Lani guessed Andy was also the one giving the signal for whatever would be waiting for them when they stepped into Rowdy Roost. The scent of evergreen and cinnamon drifted their way, blending with mouth-watering aromas from the kitchen, although it was empty of food and people.

The house was amazingly quiet considering more than thirty people were likely waiting in the old-fashioned Western bar Desiree had created a few years ago. Only the kitchen and a hallway separated them from Rowdy Roost, and those swinging bar doors didn't block sound very well.

"I like the looks of what you brought to the party." Andy helped hold the manuscripts while they each took off coats, hats, and in Granny's case, mittens. "These will be popular."

"Couples will have to share," Rance said.

"That makes Dez and me special."

Rance smiled. "Exactly."

"I'd offer to carry some of these, but I get the impression you three want to do it."

"Tis my honor to be carryin' a stack of 'em," Granny said. "I know somethin' about the labor involved."

"My hat's off to you," Andy said. "Keeping Rance's secret all these weeks."

"Not mine ta tell."

"Have you read it yet?"

"Got a good start."

"I'm about two-thirds through. Can't wait to finish it." He looked at Rance. "Impressive job, son."

"Thank you. That's—" His voice caught. "That's high praise. You read a lot."

"I do. And I'm excited for you, excited to watch your progress over the years. I would have loved to be around for the start of your mother's career, and now I get to be in on the beginning of yours. It's a privilege. I—" His phone pinged and he gave them a sheepish grin. "We're wanted in the Roost."

"Please tell me they're not going to dump a bucket of ice water on my head."

"They're not. It was discussed and Mav pitched a fit. That little girl is very protective of her Uncle Rance."

"I'll be sure to thank her."

"That said, you need to be the first one through the door." He gestured toward the kitchen, a shortcut to Rowdy Roost.

Rance gazed at him. "Is it warm water, then? I don't want to get these manuscripts wet."

"Nothing liquid will fall on you, I promise."

"That leaves a lot of possibilities still open." He handed his stack to Andy. "Hang onto these until I make it through whatever's in store for me." He started through the kitchen.

Andy motioned for Lani to go next, then Granny. He brought up the rear.

"I take it Beau was involved in this?" Rance called over his shoulder.

"What do you think?"

"There's my answer. Considering all the pranks I've pulled, I deserve whatever he's come up with."

"Mav and Zach helped."

"Is that supposed to be comforting?"

"Beau calls it passing the torch."

"Oh, boy."

When they entered the hallway leading to the swinging bar doors, the perfect silence was broken by rustling and whispers. A child giggled and was quickly shushed.

Rance paused in front of the louvered doors.

"Hold on," Andy murmured. "Granny, go on up with Lani so you can see." He moved in behind the two of them. "Okay, we're set."

Rance let out a nervous chuckle. "Here goes." Pushing through, he yelped as balloons of all colors rained down amid cheers and laughter.

But not just balloons. Lani held open one door and Andy held the other, which wasn't easy when they were laughing so hard. Plush animals followed the balloons, bouncing off Rance's head, shoulders and arms. Bears, tigers, monkeys, dogs, kitties, rabbits and a couple she couldn't identify descended from above and created a menagerie at his feet, except for a snake that dangled from his shoulder Then a small turtle plopped down with just the right trajectory to land on his head. And stay there.

As the group clapped and cheered, Beau stepped up brandishing a confetti cannon.

Rance sighed. "C'mon, bro. I'll end up with it in my—"

Beau glanced over his shoulder at the noisy group. "Should I spare him?"

A roar of *noooo* sealed the deal.

"Gotta do it, little brother. The people have spoken." Grinning, he aimed the black tube a couple feet over Rance's head. With a dramatic *boom*, confetti shot skyward and drifted down, covering the guest of honor in a rainbow of color. The crowd went wild.

"Wow." Lani struggled to get her breath back as she glanced at Andy. "Does this happen a lot?"

"This was more elaborate than most, but yeah, the McLintocks like to celebrate."

"Pure craic it was." Granny took a lace-trimmed handkerchief from the pocket of her dress and dabbed at her eyes. "Laughed so hard I got tears in m'eyes."

"Go on in," Andy said. "But watch your step.

"Granny, you go ahead." Lani held back to let her have a bit of the spotlight. Her parents had mentioned that Granny had been an instant hit with the little ones.

Mav broke from the crowd and charged toward Rance, arms outstretched. Zach followed, also aiming for Rance until he caught sight of Granny. Then he changed course.

Lani edged into the room just as Rance scooped Mav into his arms. "You did this?"

"We did, Uncle Rance! Uncle Rrrrance, Rance, Rance!" She giggled and plucked the turtle off his head. "Look! It's Squirt!" She waved the toy in his face and continued to jabber at top speed.

Meanwhile Granny leaned down to greet Zach, who stared up at her, his gaze adoring. "Hiya, lad. Did ya help make all this?"

He nodded. "That's my snake." He pointed to the plush reptile still hanging from Rance's shoulder. "His name's Jack. And that's my monkey, and that's my kitty, and that's— oh, no, here come Susie and Jodi. They'll try to take my stuff."

"We can't have that, can we, boyo?" Granny looked up. "Can ya hold these for a minute, Lani? I have business ta take care of."

"Sure thing." She balanced Granny's stack on top of her own.

"I'll take some." Andy relieved her of several. "You need to see this. That woman's the best arbitrator I've ever met. Zach's a bit shy and those two little girls, Susie and Jodi, go after his toys. Granny's showing him how to stand up for himself without getting into a fight with them."

"That's awesome." While the adults converged on Rance and Mav, Granny quietly redistributed the plush toys so that the two girls had what was theirs while Zack had a pile of his and Mavs. It sounded like she was using different voices to make each of the animals talk, which turned frowns and scowls to smiles and giggles. "Do you know she used to be a teacher?"

"I do. I'll bet she was terrific. She understands kids."

"Not only kids. People. But I also just discovered there's a will of iron under that sweet smile."

Andy chuckled. "Tried to argue with her, did you? I've—"

"Hey, there, you two." Beau strolled over. "It appears you have the goods. Need help distributing those manuscripts?"

"Thanks." Lani instinctively put a protective hand over the stack. "We'd better find out how Rance wants to do it."

"Perfect." He looked over at his brother. "Hey there, bro! When do we get our books?"

Rance flashed him a grin. "Oh, so the man who's responsible for putting confetti in my Jockeys wants a book? Fancy that."

"I voted against the cannon." Jess followed her husband over, Mav's three-month old baby brother Drew cuddled against her chest in a sling. "Can I please have a book?"

"'Yes, ma'am." Rance gave Mav a kiss on the cheek and set her on her feet. "Gotta pass out the books, sweetheart."

"Can I help?"

"Don't see why not."

"Zach wants to help, too." She turned around. "Zach! Come help!" Then she looked up at Rance as the little boy trotted over. "He needs his snake."

"Oh, right. Here you go, buddy." He took it off his shoulder and draped it around Zach's neck. Then he relieved Lani of her stack. "Thank you for holding these." His warm gaze met hers.

Her breath caught and she wobbled a bit. Even covered in confetti, he was the sexiest man she'd ever met. When he gave her that look, she went up in flames. And she'd do whatever it took to spend one more night lost in his arms.

23

Would Lani engineer a way to hitch a ride home with him? During the hours that followed, the question popped into Rance's head every time he scanned the room to see what she was up to, who she was talking with, and whether that could be the conversation that did the trick.

By eight-thirty, the party was winding down. Even Sam was curled up on his bed in the corner. And still no sign that Lani had achieved her goal.

Currently she was on the far side of the room with his mom and Andy while they admired three-month-old Matthew McLintock. After sleeping through most of the festivities in his bassinet, Marsh and Ella's son had decided to join the party.

From his vantage point Rance could only see tiny fists waving in the air, but judging from the smiles of the adults, Matty was putting on a good show. The other three-month-old, Mav's baby brother Drew, had been whisked away when all the couples with toddlers had headed out nearly an hour ago.

Before she'd gone home, Mav had asked if he'd like to keep Squirt as a souvenir. She'd looked immensely relieved when he'd told her Squirt would be lonesome without his friends.

What a kid. He was nuts about her, nuts about all of them. Did Lani want kids? It wasn't a good question to ask, all things considered.

But he hadn't factored in an additional punch to the gut if she rejected him, as she was determined to do. Someday she might show up at Rowdy Ranch with a husband, which would be torture enough. But in years to come, she might also arrive with some adorable munchkins....

"Your turn, bro." Lucky gave him a nudge.

"Right, right." He brought his attention back to the three-way dart game in which Kieran was, as usual, kicking their butts. "Sorry."

"No worries. Kieran's over by the bar gabbing with Sara, Angie and Oksana. I seem to be the only one focused on this game."

"Everybody's getting tired."

"Or crushing on their future editor."

"Now that would be dumb, wouldn't it?" He fired off his first dart. Didn't land quite where he wanted it.

"It would, but sex can make us stupid. I'm thinking you had more than one motive for handing Lani your manuscript."

"No comment." His second dart hit the bullseye. That was more like it. Then he screwed up his third throw, which meant he had no chance unless Kieran suddenly forgot how to play. He retrieved his darts.

"It's a helluva book, Rance."

"You've finished it? How could you possibly—"

"I'm fast, but not that fast. I've read enough to know it has the potential to be big."

"That's great news." He gazed at his brother. "It's not a sideline. I want to make a living at this."

"You have the chops."

"Good to hear. Especially from my favorite bookseller."

"The concept's dynamite and you execute it well. I just...."

"What?"

"I have a new perspective on the book business after watching the rise of indie authors and listening to Trent's views on marketing."

"Mom's thinking about trying it."

"I know. We've talked. I'm excited about it for her, and now Oksana's considering that route."

"But why? She just got her foot in the door."

"And she sees it'll take years to build a following because the publisher's holding her to one book a year, or at the most, every eight months. That's their model."

"That's how Mom's schedule is and she's been okay with it."

"I'm not sure she is anymore. Ebooks have changed things. Print can still work, but not like it used to."

"I believe you, but I still can't wait to see *Tequila Shots* on a bookstore shelf."

"If you went indie, it could be on a shelf in L'Amour and More by February."

"And only there."

Lucky smiled. "You wanna be in the airport."

"Yeah. Probably not realistic for a first book, but someday."

"I get it, bro. But I predict that dream's gonna take a while and they'll pay you peanuts. Trent could put together a marketing plan and sell the heck out of *Tequila Shots* and you'd keep a bigger chunk of the profits."

"Even if I changed my mind, I've already given it to Lani as a submission to Square Glasses Press."

"Has she told them yet?"

He shook his head. "Everybody's on Christmas break, but it doesn't matter. I'm not going back on what I said to her."

"Okay." Lucky shrugged. "It's totally your call." He turned toward the group over by the bar. "Kieran? Got time for three perfect throws?"

Kieran wandered over, grinning. "Givin' up, are ya?"

"It's reverse psychology," Rance said. "You'll try too hard. Guaranteed you'll choke."

"I might, yeah." Then he proceeded to hit the bullseye three times. "Or not."

"And that's a wrap." Ordinarily Rance would be more invested in the outcome of the game but his mind was elsewhere. Another glance across the room told him Lani was still talking to his mom and Andy.

Kieran retrieved his darts and turned toward Lucky. "Hey, y'know that fella Adam

Bridger, the one who's takin' Sara's M.R. Morrison tour tomorrow?"

"Is that the guy who wants us to open a bookstore in Mustang Valley?"

"Yeah."

"He left a voicemail for me at the shop. I didn't have time to get back to him, though."

"Well, Sara also gave the fella Angie's number since he talked about restorin' an old Victorian for the bookshop. He left Angie a voicemail, too. He wants to meet her after the tour."

"Wait." Lucky frowned. "Is he offering to pay for the renovation of that old house?"

"Sounds like it. Must be rich. I'd love to get my mitts on a Victorian. Ireland's jammers with 'em."

"I'm confused," Rance said. "Some dude who's going on Sara's tour wants you to open a third bookshop?"

"That's what he said in the voicemail. He's a big fan of Mom's books and he thinks L'Amour and More would do well in Mustang Valley"

"Hm. It's close as the crow flies but if you're not a crow...."

Lucky nodded. "You gotta go up and around Missoula. Unless you take the shortcut through the mountains."

"The widow maker." Rance shuddered. "I drove it once. Got the gray hairs to prove it. As Kieran would say, what the feck?"

"Accordin' to Sara, they're gonna fix that road soon," Kieran said. "That could put Mustang Valley on the map. Could be a grand opportunity for L'Amour and More."

"Or they don't fix the road and Lucky's left holding the bag."

Lucky punched him lightly on the arm. "Where's your spirit of adventure? Where's the can-do Rance we all know and love?"

"Sorry. I've got a lot on my mind."

Lucky's grin faded and his jaw tightened. "We've got your back, bro. We're all—hey, Lani, how's it going?"

Rance turned in surprise. How had he missed her approach? Usually his Lani radar kicked in.

She gave him a quick glance before focusing on Lucky. "I've had a wonderful time. Great party. Sorry to barge in, but I was just talking with Desiree and Andy about the book and there's a scene we all agree needs tweaking, so—"

"Don't say what it is." Lucky took a step back, palms up. "I want to read it all before I hear a word about it."

"Yeah, Lani, don't get specific." Hot damn. Looked like she was setting the stage.

"I won't. I came over to give you a heads up before I forgot. In fact, I wrote down the page numbers." She pulled a folded piece of paper from her pocket. "But as I was walking over here, suddenly the whole scene played in my head like a movie clip."

And there it was. The excuse and his cue. He didn't have to fake his excitement. "Yeah? And you think it works?"

"I think so."

"Sure wish I had my laptop handy. I could make notes on my phone but it would be better if I had the manuscript in front of me."

"D'ya want the copy you gave Sara and me t'make notes on? I'd hafta ask her but I think she'd say sure."

"Thanks, but I'd rather not mark up your copy. I think better with my fingers on the keys." He didn't look at Lani. One misstep and the whole shebang would crash and burn.

"I'm the same," she said. "I didn't think this through. I mean, you're in the middle of a celebration, and here I'm—"

"Hey, I'm glad you did and I don't want you to lose that image you have in your head." He doubted it was a scene from his book. "It's almost Granny's bedtime anyway. Would you be willing to ride over to the cabin with us?"

"I could do that."

Her super casual tone was so perfect he almost lost it. "Excellent. That way we can work from the master file. I promise I won't keep you long." He clenched his jaw to keep from grinning.

"Sounds good. I'm ready to pack it in, too." She smothered a yawn.

Or what looked like a yawn. More likely a swallowed laugh. Her high school drama training had served her well. "Then I'll go find Granny and we'll be off."

Just his luck Granny was playing poker with Buck, Marybeth and Lani's folks. He quickly explained the situation and found out Lani's folks were getting ready to leave, too.

"I don't know how much time we'll need to spend on the manuscript." He busied himself helping Granny out of her chair so he didn't have to look Harry and Vanessa in the eye while he spun the tall tale. "But it shouldn't take long."

"Don't worry about it." Harry waved a dismissive hand. "It's not like we'll wait up for her."

Just what he wanted to hear. "Then we'll see you all later."

"Oh, and Rance," Vanessa said. "Granny gave us the lowdown on Irving Quick and we're there for any backup you need."

"Thank you. I appreciate that so much."

"He'd better behave himself." Harry shared a glance with Buck. "Right?"

"That's for sure." Buck sat up straighter and his hand closed into a fist. "Although I almost want him to step out of line and give me an excuse."

Rance blinked. "To punch him?"

"It wouldn't be my first choice, but it's on the list."

That shocked him. To his knowledge Buck had never raised a hand to any human or animal. Maybe Buck had decided Irving didn't fit either category.

"I doubt he'll be a problem, but it's good to know you have my back." With a smile and a wave, he hustled Granny away from the table. Lani met them halfway, and they all called out their thanks and goodbyes as they left through the swinging bar doors.

None of them spoke as they bundled up, stepped out on the porch and closed the door behind them.

"Keep going," Rance murmured, taking Granny's left arm while Lani took her right. "We're not out of the woods yet." He had no trouble from Lani as he loaded Granny in the back while Lani hopped in the front.

When he'd finally buckled himself in and switched on the engine, he let out a sigh. Made it.

Then Granny started to giggle. "Grand craic that was! Good on ya both. Ya make a solid team, don'tcha now?"

He didn't dare agree with that assessment. Glancing over at Lani, he smiled. "You were terrific. I just followed where you led."

She flushed. "I'll admit I surprised myself."

"Not me. I knew you could do it. I just wasn't sure how."

"Neither was I. Then I started walking toward you and it came to me."

"That you'd pretend to have a vision of the scene?"

"I wasn't pretending. I really do have an idea for how that scene should go. I want to talk about it before I forget."

"Seriously?"

"Yep. The minute we get there, I want you to turn on your laptop."

"Okay, then." He'd hoped to be turning her on instead of his laptop, but if she wanted to work on his book, that's what they'd do. If it was a love scene, so much the better.

24

In the end, Lani's half-assed plan had worked, but not before taking some fascinating twists and turns. It required her to draw Desiree into a conversation about Rance's book when no one was around.

But she'd nearly given up on finding a private moment. She'd spent almost no time with Desiree until she'd gone over to admire Ella and Marsh's adorable baby. Then little Matty had jump-started her plan by filling his pants.

His parents had taken him back to the kids' wing to change him, leaving her alone with Desiree and Andy. She hadn't figured on involving Andy in analyzing a sex scene. But he'd turned out to be a terrific brainstormer, beautifully complimenting Desiree's insights.

Ella and Marsh came back with Matty before they'd found that elusive something that would take the scene from good to great. She'd volunteered to tell Rance the scene could use punching up.

But that alone wasn't enough to guarantee she'd end up in his cabin tonight. Instead, she'd pretend an amazing vision had just popped into her head and she didn't want to lose track of it. He'd take it from there.

To her surprise, a potential revision had come to her, the kind that sent a zing of excitement down her spine. As Rance navigated the dark road back to his cabin, she focused on how she saw the scene playing out.

She looked forward to his lovemaking, but she also cared about his book. Now that she'd dreamed up some alternate dialogue for the scene, she needed to get it out of her head and into the document, assuming he liked it, too. If that made her a book nerd, so be it.

The glow of Christmas lights greeted them as Rance parked in front of the cabin. Lani unbuckled her seatbelt and climbed out, eager to help Granny down so they could get this show on the road.

She opened the back door. "We're here, Granny."

Nothing. Then a soft snore.

Rance came up behind her. "What's the—"

"She's asleep."

"I wondered. She's hardly ever that quiet. Let me get her out. The front door's unlocked. If you'll go open it, I'll carry her in."

"I'll turn down her covers, too."

"Thanks. She might wake up when I haul her out, but having her bed ready is a good idea."

"I'm on it." She hurried toward the cabin, mindful of the icy steps and porch as she made her way to the door. Would Rance have any trouble navigating them while carrying Granny?

Warmth poured through the door when she opened it. After securing it with a doorstop, she raced for Granny's room, tossed back the covers and ran back to the front door.

Rance cradled a still-sleeping Granny against his chest as he eyed the porch steps.

"They're slippery. Can I do anything?"

"There's a bucket of ash on the hearth. I'll feel better making the climb if you'd pour a bunch on the steps. I've tried to wake her but she's down for the count."

"Be right back." She quickly located the bucket and returned.

"Just toss it down the middle." He moved away.

She aimed for the bottom step first, then worked her way to the top. After emptying the bucket , she glanced up. "How's that?"

"Perfect. You're hired. I need one more favor, though. There's a stack of old towels in my workout room. I need you to lay towels along the path to Granny's room. This stuff will stick to my boots and I don't want ash on my hardwood floors."

"Will do." Moving fast, she found the towels. She had two laid down when a steady thump, thump on the steps signaled he was on his way.

She'd made it into Granny's bedroom when his measured tread told her he was safely inside. She put down a couple towels crossways on one side of Granny's bed in case he needed to maneuver as he lowered her to the mattress.

When she walked out of the bedroom, he was coming her way. She moved to the far side of the hall to give him plenty of space. "I'll get the front door."

"Thanks."

By the time she returned, he'd laid her on the bed and worked her out of her coat.

"She really is a deep sleeper."

"I wonder if she took out her hearing aids."

"That could explain it."

Setting her shoes by the bed, he glanced over his shoulder. "Any chance you'd be willing to take over? At least get her out of this dress?"

"Sure."

He straightened with a sigh of relief and turned toward her. "If you weren't here I'd man up and do it."

"But I am." She smiled. "Go turn on your laptop. It's the scene where Sophia seduces Dooley."

His expression brightened. "That's what you want to work on?"

"Yes."

"Nice." He toed off his boots and picked them up. "Did I mention that I like writing in bed?"

"You did, but we're not handling this revision in your bed."

"Spoilsport."

"I'll borrow a chair from the kitchen or we can move to the kitchen table. We're keeping things professional."

"It'll be more comfortable on my bed and I'm more creative there."

"I'm aware."

"That's not what I meant."

"We'd never make it through the scene."

"We would, I promise. We'll keep our clothes on until it's done."

"I don't think that's a—"

"Ya should listen to Rance." Granny pushed herself to a sitting position. "Knows what he's doin', he does."

Lani burst out laughing. "Granny! Have you been playing possum?"

"I've never heard of that game, luv."

"It's an animal that's good at playing dead," Rance said. "I don't think you have them in Ireland. How long have you been awake?"

"Not fer long. Woke up durin' this interestin' debate yer havin'. Musta drifted off comin' home." She peered at Rance. "Ya had to carry me in, didn'tcha?"

"It was my privilege."

"Yer a good boy." She glanced at the towels on the floor. "Jaysus! What's that mess?"

"Fireplace ash. No worries. We'll get 'em cleaned up. We put ash on the steps to make sure I didn't slip on the ice." He rolled the towels together and tucked them under his arm.

"Didn't mean ta make trouble fer ya, lad."

"I would sacrifice every towel in this cabin if it means keeping you safe."

Her gaze softened. "I know ya would. Warms the cockles of m'heart, it does. Now go on with ya. Work on yer book." She glanced at Lani. "He'll keep his word, ya know. He always does."

"I do and I will. Nothing happens until we're satisfied with that scene. I wrote it in bed in the first place. It's part of my process." He delivered the explanation straight. No wink or sly grin.

Clearly he believed the revisions would go better if they sat propped up on his king-sized bed. And when they were done, well... they wouldn't have to change venues, would they?

She was stirred up by the prospect, and judging from the gleam in his eyes, so was he. If he needed a certain setting for inspiration, who was she to argue? "Alrighty." She slipped off her coat. "Trade you my coat for those towels. If you have a place I can put them to soak, I'll—"

"I'll handle it."

"Let her do it, lad. Ya need to get yer laptop goin'. Lani, use the big sink in the laundry. Tis off the kitchen."

"Perfect." She plucked the towels from under Rance's arm and handed him her coat. "I'll go get the others. See you in your bedroom in five minutes."

25

    Rance kept his rolltop desk closed out of habit. He tended to write random bits about his story on slips of paper. He hadn't wanted anyone to see those scattered notes in case they'd guess what he was up to.

    Didn't matter anymore. After sliding back the cover to take out his laptop, he left it open and headed for his bedroom.

    Felt weird not to be hiding this project and even more strange to think of twenty-plus copies circulating among his family members. Eventually the book would end up in the hands of strangers.

    He alternated between the thrill of having an audience and the terror of being vulnerable. But there was no terror when it came to Lani. He wanted her to see him, to have all the information.

    If she hadn't liked this book... but she had, more than he'd dared hope. Tonight they'd dive into a new experience, rewriting a section of it with her input. That excited him. Not as much as the promise of making love afterward, but he wanted this experience, too.

    Ditching the idea of having something to drink while they worked, he began setting up. He switched on the fireplace, choosing glowing embers. He left the comforter pulled up and stacked pillows against the headboard.

Last of all he picked up his favorite pillow, climbed in and balanced the laptop on it. Both firm and fat, it was better than any lap desk he'd tried.

He'd opened the book file and was scrolling to find the sex scene when the tap of Lani's boot heels sent a jolt of excitement through his body. The soft click of his door closing made his cock twitch in anticipation.

He kept his eyes on the screen and took a deep breath. He could do this. It would be fun, assuming he could focus on the work.

She paused at the foot of the bed. "I see what you mean."

"About what?" He glanced up. And longed to grab her.

"Your process. Sitting at a desk isn't you."

"I tried it. Mom writes at a desk. I even have her same view of the mountains through that window." He was pleased with his conversational tone considering he was on fire. "Then one night I brought my laptop in here and now I mostly use the desk to hide the evidence."

She smiled. "I saw your piles of notes."

"Top secret. Or it was." He gestured toward the empty spot next to him. "Come on in. I've never had a writing partner. I want to see what it's like." And he'd test his willpower to the max.

"Just remember it's your book." She walked around the bed and propped her shapely tush on the mattress while she took off her boots. "You don't have to use my idea."

"I'll keep that in mind." The more he stuffed in his head the less room he'd have for lustful impulses.

Swinging her sock-clad feet up on the bed she scooted back. "Your mom and Andy are good brainstormers. They might come up with something better. We ran out of time." Adjusting the pillows, she shoved one behind her head and leaned against it.

"You discussed this section with them?" He'd missed that part of the scheme.

"Yeah." She grinned. "Andy's hilarious, and wow, do those two know their stuff. We bounced ideas around just like I do with my buddies at Square Glasses."

"Andy's sharp. Mom says between him and the Wenches, she gets great feedback."

Lani turned her head and met his gaze. "I forgot that all the Wenches have the book now. Will they give you notes?"

"Probably. I asked them to." He wanted to kiss her. All over. "We should get started."

"Yes." She swallowed. "I've never talked about revisions face-to-face with an author."

"How do you usually handle it?"

"In an email. Sometimes on the phone."

"We could grab our phones if that would make you more comfortable."

"We tried talking about the book on the phone the other night, remember?"

"I remember everything, Lani-lou." And he might have just screwed up his favorite writing routine. Every time he brought his laptop into the bedroom, he'd picture her nestled against the pillows, her cheeks flushed, her eyes bright, her body eager for his.

He made himself look down at the screen. "Ready to do this?"

"Yep." She gestured to the laptop. "Where are you?"

"They're in the bar. He's just hung up the closed sign and she's flirting with him like crazy." He shifted the pillow so she could see better.

She inched a little closer, bringing her sweet scent with her. "I love their banter here. Her decision to start backing up the stairs and coaxing him to follow is so much fun."

"Glad you like it." Her praise, delivered in a slightly breathless voice, sent a message straight to his cock. He sent a message back. *Stay down.* "He's trying to talk her out of it."

"Which fits his character, to lay out his bad track record in detail. But Sophia's a rescuer, a fixer."

"That's why she counters with *I don't care.*"

"Yeah, but what if, instead of saying she doesn't care, each time she says *I know.*"

"Why would she know?"

"Because she's a cop!"

"Small-town sheriff."

"Close enough. And because she's a cop, before she ever makes a move on this guy, she investigates the hell out of him. I think readers will like that she did that."

"She looked into his background enough to find out he used to be a deputy."

"But that was work related. She needed his help with cases. When her interest became personal, she dug deeper. She's been burned before."

"She has." He'd resisted the suggestion, but now he got it. "She would want more info." He began changing Sophia's responses from *don't care* to *I know.*

"And then, when she has him where she wants him—"

"Which is?"

"Here." She pointed to the line.

Dooley gave up. With a groan of surrender, he thrust deep.

Rance's breath caught as a sharp pain told him his cock was not happy. He gave it a talking to. "Okay, what happens then besides the obvious?" Not sounding so casual now, was he?

"I have another piece of dialogue if you want to hear it."

"You bet."

"Before they continue, Dooley says *Is there anything you don't know about me?* And she says *I don't know if you're any good in the sack.* And he says—"

"Time to finish your investigation."

"Yes! Exactly!"

He grinned as he continued to type. "I like it. A lot. Thanks."

"Anytime."

If only she meant that. He finished making the changes, hit Save and turned the screen her way. "Want to take a look?"

"Later."

Her sultry tone caught his attention. *Oh, yeah.* The sizzle of passion in her eyes warmed him all over, especially the area below his belt. Closing the laptop, he laid it on the nightstand and tossed the pillow to the floor. "Much later."

26

Lani left the bed and started ripping off her clothes. So did Rance. Their frenzied efforts made her laugh. "Is this a contest?"

"Yes, ma'am. First one naked gets to choose the position." He yanked his partially unbuttoned shirt over his head.

She didn't care who was where as long as he found a way to relieve the ache deep in her core. Reading his sexy words while snuggled close to his tempting body had created a need that wouldn't be denied.

But she never could resist a challenge. When she tossed away her bra and unfastened her jeans, he totally lost his place in the game. Victory was in her grasp as his motions slowed and his hungry gaze swept over her.

"Hey, there, slowpoke."

Blinking, he quickly unbuckled his belt, but it was too late to catch up.

She kicked away her jeans and pulled off her socks. Smiling in triumph, she savored her front-row view of Rance McLintock taking off his pants.

She didn't consider herself shallow. She prized inner beauty over outer. But when a man was built like Rance, ignoring his attributes would be like refusing to look at a spectacular sunrise.

Her breath caught when he ditched his briefs and stood before her gloriously naked and aroused. Going down this path was risky, but he was worth it.

"Go ahead and climb in." He pulled open the nightstand drawer. "I need to make sure we don't procreate."

"Yeah, that would be a game changer."

"It would." He held her gaze, not for long, but long enough for an ache to settle into her womb.

He'd be the kind of dad who'd call his kids munchkins, who'd get down on the floor with them, blow raspberries on their bellies, pick them up and dance around the room, laughing as they squealed with joy.

She pictured him climbing into bed without a condom, eager to create a baby. He'd make beautiful ones. The ache in her womb was joined by an ache in her heart.

"What do you want?" His soft murmur was close, very close.

She opened her eyes. When had she closed them? "You." Her throat wasn't working right. She cleared it. "I want you."

He smiled. "You won." Dipping his head, he brushed his mouth over hers. "I have to keep my kisses light so my bristle doesn't give you a rash, but other than that, anything goes. You get to choose how you want me."

Her throat tightened. Why did he have to be so sweet and sexy? Why did he have to be so absolutely perfect? "Just... just love me."

He lifted his head, his gaze searching hers. "Did I say the wrong thing a minute ago?"

"About what?"

"Making sure we don't procreate. Introducing something we haven't—"

"It's okay."

"If I touched a nerve, I'm sorry."

"The thing is, I want to have kids."

A flash of pain in his eyes was quickly doused. "And I'm sure you will."

"I want yours."

His eyes widened.

"I know that's messed up. I saw you with those little cutie-pies and of course you'll have your own and I won't be the—"

"Shh." He dropped a soft kiss on her lips. "It'll be okay." Moving over her, he eased between her thighs, rocked his hips and made the connection she craved. So easy. So elemental. So right.

She held on, wrapping him in her arms as she rose to meet him and focused on just this moment. And the next, and the next.

Holding her gaze, he gently built tension stroke by stroke. "Any requests?"

"Don't stop."

"Not gonna." His breathing roughened. "You've got me where you want me, Lani-lou. I'll stay as long as you need me to."

She lost herself in his eyes — dark, intense, fully engaged.

"We'll figure this out." He increased the pace. "You don't believe me, but we will."

She didn't believe him. But she believed in this. Tightening her grip on his sweat-slicked body, she hovered on the edge of a climax. There. A ripple. Almost....

With a gasp, he bore down.

Her world exploded, wrenching a sharp cry from her throat. Powerful waves of release tossed her like a toy boat in a hurricane. She clung to him, calling his name.

"I'm here." His low-pitched words ended in a shout of triumph. Pushing deep, he let go, gulping for air. His body shook in response to the strong pulse of his cock as it bestowed the most intimate caress of all.

She reveled in the sensation, breathing in his scent. She wanted more of it, longed to bury her nose in the curve of his neck.

As his breathing slowed, she pressed gently on his back. "Come down here."

He resisted. "I'm sweaty. And heavy."

"I like sweaty. I'm not asking you to drop like a stone. Just come closer."

He eased down until his soft chest hair tickled her skin.

"More. Press down a little. Rest your head on my shoulder."

His mouth tilted up in a half-smile. "Found your mojo, did you?"

"I like how you smell, okay?"

He chuckled. "I don't hear that very often." Easing down until his pecs pressed lightly against her breasts, he laid his head on her shoulder. "For the record, I like how you smell, too. Especially now."

"That's lovely to hear." She stroked his damp hair back from his forehead and sighed. "Why do you have to smell like the man who should father my babies?"

"For the same reason you smell like the woman who should have my babies. Pheromones."

"I thought that was nonsense."

"Guess not." He nestled closer. "At least now you know what to look for. Or sniff out."

"It's not that easy. I've never had this reaction before."

"Backatcha."

"It's a cruel joke played by Mother Nature."

"You don't believe we can fix this."

"I don't. Your determination is sexy, but it's unrealistic."

"If you think my determination is sexy, wait til you get a load of my ingenuity. You'll want to jump my bones on the spot."

"I'm sure I will."

"Thinking my way out of tight spots is my superpower." Raising his head, he gazed at her. "I need to abandon this cozy bed and take care of business. Don't go away."

"Not likely, since I'd have to swipe your truck."

"You know what I mean."

"Yeah, I do." He didn't want her to get dressed and announce it was time to go. "I'll be here."

"Good." He left the bed and headed for his bathroom.

He wasn't kidding about his ingenuity. The next three nights were taken, but her plane didn't leave until New Year's Day. Guaranteed he'd find more excuses for them to be alone between Christmas and her departure.

What then? She'd fly home with her memories and the latest version of his manuscript. Square Glasses would buy it. She had her pitch ready and Sasha respected her judgment.

Rance would become her author, beginning a business relationship that would last as long as he stayed with Square Glasses. Being sensible adults, they'd downgrade their personal connection from lovers to friends.

Yeah, right. As he walked out of the bathroom looking like every woman's fantasy, she made a command decision.

Scooting up into a sitting position, she faced him. "This isn't gonna work."

27

"What isn't?" Rance knew exactly what Lani was talking about but he needed to buy time. The pleasure they'd shared had turned his brain to jelly. He'd expected her to say something like this eventually, but not right after great sex. Evidently her recovery time was shorter than his.

"You going with Square Glasses. Becoming my author."

His chest hollowed out. "You don't want me?" Still stalling for time, he said it teasingly as he climbed back into bed and mirrored her position.

"You know I do. I want you desperately. That's the problem. When I leave here, it will be the end of this." She made a vague gesture that encompassed his package and her lady parts.

"We'll both lose our sex drive?"

"You're making fun of me."

"Sorry." He took a breath. "I joke around when I'm terrified. It's a bad habit."

Her expression softened. "I'm sorry, too. But you can't be my author. In our company that's a special relationship. We're encouraged to build a strong bond and create mutual trust."

He took both her hands. "And we've done that already. We're ahead of the game."

"But we broke the rules of that game. We became lovers. Maybe you'll be okay communicating regularly, knowing we'll never again be—"

"How can you say never?"

"Because it makes no sense! We'll see each other at most three times a year and maybe less than that. Face the facts."

Did she want to be free of him? His chest hurt. "When you say I should face facts, does that mean you want to start dating when you get home?"

"Of course not. It'll take me a while to...." She glanced away. "Let's just say you won't be easy to get over."

That helped. He let out a breath. "You said you might come for Easter."

"I probably can." She glanced back at him, her eyes filled with sadness. "It'll be a short visit."

He held her gaze. "Then what if we don't make any big decisions now? Why don't we wait and see how things go when we're separated?"

"We'll only be delaying the inevitable."

"Works for me." He made himself say the next part. "And if, sometime before Easter, you meet someone, then you should go for it."

Her throat moved in a slow swallow. "Okay. Same goes for you."

He smiled. "It won't happen."

"Probably not for me, either, so come next April, we'll be in the same fix we are now, only your book will be in production at Square Glasses. That will be a done deal. That's what worries me."

He was beginning to get the picture. If he wasn't with her publisher, they'd have no reason to keep in touch. They'd only see each other when she visited the ranch. But once he signed a contract with Square Glasses, they'd be communicating regularly... perhaps for years.

Only one thing to do. "Don't take the manuscript back with you this time. Wait until Easter."

"That's crazy. You'll lose almost four months. If I submit it as soon as I get back, they can get you into the fall schedule. If I wait until April, it won't come out until the following year."

"So what? It buys us another four months to find a way to be together. No telling what could happen between now and then."

"I'll tell you what'll happen. You'll miss getting a book out during the holidays. That was another idea I had that I haven't mentioned yet. You've set this in November. It wouldn't take much to switch to December and add some references to Christmas. You'll increase sales if you do that."

"It's not a Christmas book."

"It could be. If *Die Hard* is a Christmas movie, anything goes."

"So it comes out a year from this fall. No worries."

"Rance, do you hear yourself? You're twisting your writing career into a pretzel because of me. I won't have it. The obvious solution is to take it to another publisher."

His whole body tightened. "I don't want to."

"I'm not talking about your mom's or any of the big ones. I can recommend another small press. I know the people there."

In a typical Lani move, she'd made a logical suggestion, one that could save them potential heartbreak. And he hated it. "No."

"It's the reasonable—"

"What about your publisher? You seem to think my book will sell. Won't they miss out on an opportunity?"

"I've wrestled with that, but the owner will understand the potential problems given our personal relationship. Besides, we likely wouldn't keep you long. You'll get a better offer and—"

"I wouldn't take it."

"Because of me? You'd throw away—"

"Yes, dammit! I've pictured you as my editor from the first words I typed. I don't want anyone else messing with—"

"Then you *did* write it for me."

"Okay, I did! You're my muse, my inspiration to finally get off my butt and do the thing I've known was my calling since I was eight years old! Happy now?"

"Of course I'm not happy." She gulped. "You've put us both in a no-win situation."

"Me? What about—"

"You're right! I'm guilty, too! But for your own good, please consider my suggestion."

"Thanks, but no thanks."

"I can refuse to submit it to Square Glasses."

"That's your choice. If you don't do it this time, I'll ask again in April."

"Rance! For God's sake, don't—"

"Maybe I should take you home." Before he said anything else, things he could never take back.

"Good idea." She scrambled off the bed.

He moved a little slower, weighed down by a despair heavier than he'd ever known. This plan had dazzled him from its inception. He'd never doubted that he and Lani would end up together. How could he have gotten it so wrong?

28

Lani didn't sleep worth a damn and woke up in a foul mood. She desperately needed to share this fustercluck with the only one who wouldn't freak out, but Sara was guiding a tour today. It was the last one before suspending them until after New Year's.

She picked up her phone to check the time. Sara wouldn't have left yet. She sent a quick text asking if she had time to talk when she got back.

Hey, there! I do, but why not go on the tour with me? I just had a cancellation. We can talk on the way into town and then you can find out what your little sis is up to. I'll come get you in the van.

She sighed in relief. What a great distraction from her negative thoughts. She texted back an enthusiastic response and headed for the shower.

A couple of minutes before Sara was due, she bundled up and went out on the porch. She'd informed her parents about the plan and they were delighted she was doing it. They'd taken the tour weeks ago and said it was great fun even though they already knew everything Sara told the group.

Watching her little sister pilot a ten-person van up the narrow road was a kick. Yeah, this was a great idea. Thank goodness for Sara.

Taking the porch steps as fast as she dared, she hurried around to the passenger side and hauled herself in.

Sara grinned. "Some tour director I am. I didn't put the steps out for you."

"I would have been insulted if you had. Thanks for letting me come. I'll be in charge of the steps."

"Perfect." She backed the van around with practiced ease. "I was gonna ask if you would. Sometimes a person will volunteer to sit in front and do that, which makes things go faster. Other times no one in the group is agile enough."

"I think I can handle it."

"Then you have the job. Unless Adam insists on taking. over. I'm pretty sure he's a cowboy and you know how they are."

She certainly did. "Who's Adam?"

"You didn't hear the talk last night?"

"Must have missed it."

"His name's Adam Bridger. His family has a ranch over in Mustang Valley and evidently they've done very well for themselves. He's an M.R. Morrison fan and is determined to have a branch of L'Amour and More in his town."

"Wow. How exciting that people are coming to Lucky, now."

"It really helped when Desiree uncloaked herself. The tour starts and ends at the bookstore and she'll be there to sign her latest when I bring everyone back."

"Does she always do that?"

"No. This is special, which is why Adam chose to come now. He'll make his full pitch to Lucky afterward. He told me he wanted to do that in person. Angie and Kieran will come by this afternoon, too, and Kendall if she can swing it. Adam wants to hire them to refurbish the Victorian where he wants to locate the bookstore."

"All this came up at the party last night?"

"Sure did."

"Maybe that's the conversation I interrupted when I went over to talk to Rance."

"I'm sure it was. I saw you come over, and then you took off with Rance and Granny. What was that all about?"

"Funny you should ask." Taking a deep breath, she laid out the complicated situation she'd landed herself in. They were halfway to town before she finished.

"Whoa, sis. I think you've made a bigger mess than I did when I fell for Kieran."

"It feels like it. Have you had a chance to read any of his book?"

"Kieran read me the first chapter while I was getting ready. It sounded really good."

"It is. Best first novel I've ever read. He has huge potential and he's stuck on the idea I have to be his editor. That's ridiculous."

"That's love."

Lani groaned. "I don't want to hear that."

"Because you don't love him?"

"I—"

"Don't bother denying it. Everybody knows you've been crazy about him for months. We just figured it would have to burn itself out somehow because you were so resistant."

"That's what would have happened, but then he wrote this book."

"You're right that you can't submit it to Square Glasses. If you're gonna ditch him, you can't be his editor."

"But he doesn't want anybody else."

"He'll have to get over that. I'm sure Desiree's had more than one editor in forty years."

"I'm sure she has, too. She might be able to talk some sense into him."

"I take it she doesn't know what's going on."

"She probably has some idea, but unless he's told her, she doesn't have the whole story. I don't feel right telling her, either. He hadn't admitted he wrote it for me until I made him angry enough to blurt it out. I can't see him confessing it to his mom."

"Well, you said he loved the process, and now he's announced to his whole family that this is the first book in a series. It might take a while, but he'll finally accept the idea of a different small press and a different editor."

"Yeah. He has to, but I hate that this impacts his special moment."

"Because you love him and want him to be happy."

"God help me, I do. But if I sacrifice my career to give him his, that's no good."

"I gotta hand it to you, sis. You really know how to screw up a romance."

"What do you think I should do?"

"Nothing."

"You know I'm really bad at doing nothing."

"If I had a brilliant suggestion I'd tell you, but it looks to me like anything you do will only make it worse. You've given him a solution — a different small publisher. You can even tell him which editor to send his book to."

"I already have someone in mind. She's excellent and she'd love his sense of humor."

"He can't ask for more than that."

"Well, he can, but it's the best I've come up with."

"Then you need to leave him alone and hope that he eventually sees the wisdom of your suggestion. Also, for the record, I'm sorry. You two would have made a great couple, but you're right. There's nothing in Wagon Train for you."

"Even if there was, if I give up my job at Square Glasses and move here, he loses his connection to the kind of small publisher he's looking for. There's just no way I can be the editor for his book. It was never going to work out."

Sara pulled the van into a parking space in front of L'Amour and More and shut off the engine. "Again, I'm sorry, sis. This sucks for both of you."

"You said it." She held her sister's gaze. "Thanks for listening. And for inviting me on the tour."

"We'll have fun, I promise." She glanced past Lani's shoulder. "I'll bet that's him."

"Him?"

"Adam Bridger. Definitely not a tourist."

Lani turned to peer out the window at a tall, broad-shouldered man standing outside the bookstore while he talked to a gray-haired woman in a navy parka. "That's a Montana cowboy right there."

"Imposing in an unassuming way."

"Cowboys excel at that." Adam's black Stetson shaded his face except for the firm line of his jaw. His confident, slightly bow-legged stance marked him as someone who'd spent considerable time on the back of a horse.

"Let's go meet him. I'm excited for Lucky. Adam looks like the kind of guy who makes things happen."

<u>29</u>

Rance loved Christmas at the Buffalo. Tyra and Clint went all out with lights and decorations, the band played holiday favorites and customers ordered festive drinks. It was his favorite time to be a bartender.

Not today.

But he was a professional and their clientele didn't need to be exposed to his crappy mood. He laughed and joked with everyone, including his brother Clint, who kept an eye on the bar and pitched in whenever the orders got out of control.

Clint saw through his act, of course, although he didn't say so. The occasional brotherly hand on his shoulder or a knowing glance sent his way said more than words that he understood the anxiety masked by his outward cheer.

His big brother had no idea. He likely thought Irving Quick's arrival was the problem. But his shitty dad was the least of his concerns. He'd thought he had his life figured out, and last night the whole structure had collapsed like an Eiffel Tower made of popsicle sticks.

He'd been through some bad patches in his life, most recently with Lucky back in February. They'd almost come to blows and now they were tighter than ever. February had been a watershed month. He'd emerged a changed man, one with exciting prospects that had a good chance of materializing.

Or so he'd thought. Oh, he'd been transformed, all right. He'd always been something of an idiot, or eejit, as Kieran would say. But he'd been a happy one. Not anymore. Things couldn't possibly get any worse.

Then his father strolled into the bar.

Wrong again.

Hard to miss the guy. That black turtleneck and leather jacket must be part of his brand. He could have walked right off the back of his book cover. Pretension, thy name is Irving Quick.

He sailed right past the wooden mascot as if he heard talking buffalos every day of the week.

Rance's lip curled. He might have even snarled.

"Easy, bro." Clint had silently moved to stand beside him. "Don't let this loser get to you."

"He was mean to Mom."

"I know, and he won't ever have the opportunity again."

"Damn straight. D'ya think he knows I'm here?"

"I think you're *why* he's here."

"Mom told him?"

"Doubt it. My guess is he hasn't been out there yet. All he had to do was stop someone on the street.   Everybody   in   town   knows   Rance McLintock."

That comment put a little more starch in his spine. He didn't always wear his Stetson while working behind the bar, but today he had. He tugged down the brim and straightened his shoulders.

Clint chuckled. "Attaboy."

He didn't want to look at the jerk, but he couldn't help it. This would be him in thirty years. There was no mistaking they were father and son.

Bile rose in his throat. He didn't want to look like this piece of trash. Tomorrow he'd shave his head and grow a mustache.

His   dear   old   dad   seemed   equally fascinated with him. He paused a few feet away and openly stared. "It's like looking in a mirror."

"In a fun house," Rance muttered under his breath. Then he pasted a smile on his face. "Can I help you, sir?"

"You don't recognize me?"

"Can't say I do."

He blew out a breath, clearly annoyed. "Of course you do. You had to know I was coming. I'm your father."

"Oh, that's right. Mom did say something about it. What's your name again?"

Clint snorted and went to take a drink order.

"I'm Irving Quick." He took a hardback out of   a   satchel.   "I   brought   you   a   book.   It's autographed."

"Thanks, but I don't read that stuff. You could donate it to the local library, though. They're always happy to promote struggling new authors."

"I'm not a—okay, cut the crap. You know damn well who I am. You're just pissed at me, and I get that. Let's start over."

"No can do. It's water under the dam and over the bridge."

"Oh, you're my son, all right. I was a smart-mouthed kid, too, always had the last word. You're a chip—"

"Complete that sentence and I'm coming across this bar. I'm the son of Desiree McLintock and you're nothing but a sperm donor. Got it?"

Applause erupted from a nearby table. He glanced over. In his misery he hadn't noticed several of the Wenches were having lunch at the Buffalo today. Coincidence? Likely not.

Irving didn't look pleased. Evidently he'd expected a different reception. Oh, well.

"Coming in here while you're working was a bad idea."

"Figured that out, didja?"

"Do you have a break coming up?"

"Not anytime soon."

"When does your shift end?"

"It depends."

"I haven't been out to the ranch yet and I... I was hoping before I go we could talk, man to man, maybe clear the air."

"Oh, I see. You want to absolve yourself with a ten-minute chat. What a self-absorbed concept." He turned away and picked up a bar rag. "I have work to do, so—"

"Are you writing?"

He froze. Had somebody squealed on him? No. His family wouldn't have told. Had to be a wild guess on Irving's part.

"You are! My God, that makes me happy. You have no idea. Neither of my other—well, that's not important. You're writing. That's amazing. What are you writing? No, it doesn't really matter, does it? Just the fact that—"

"Hey, Rance." Clint approached, phone in hand. "I just texted Tyra. She's coming out to help behind the bar. She'll leave the office open. You can use—"

"Thanks, but I'll pass on that offer."

Clint turned his back to Irving and lowered his voice. "You should talk to him."

"Don't want to."

"Do it anyway. It's like lancing a boil. Keeps it from festering."

"Clint..."

"It's what Mom would say."

"Damn you."

"I'll take that rag. Go make us proud."

Chest tight, he handed over the bar rag and faced Irving. "Clint's letting us use the office." Opening the hinged portion of the bar, he walked through the opening. "Follow me."

"Clint?" Irving glanced over his shoulder. "That's Clint? I never would have guessed. He and Cheyenne were such toothpicks."

"Bret and Gil's dad brought us all weights and showed us how to train. Everyone's been working out for years."

"I see."

"Marsh lets us use his punching bag whenever we want. He's into kickboxing. Damn good at it, too. So's his wife." He gave Tyra a salute as she passed them headed for the bar.

"And all you kids still live out there, I gather."

"We do. We're a tight group. One for all and all for one."

"If you're trying to scare the shit out of me, you're doing a bang-up job."

"Just telling it like it is. Don't be expecting a welcome banner strung across the front porch. Nobody's happy about your visit and some are openly hostile."

"Like you, for instance."

"You picked up on that? And here I thought I was being subtle." He paused beside the open door and gestured for Irving to go in first.

He hesitated before crossing the threshold.

Rance followed him in and closed the door. "Afraid I'll take this opportunity to work you over?"

"It crossed my mind. You have thirty-two years on me plus all that weight training. With the band playing nobody would be the wiser. I couldn't hear what Clint said to you. For all I know he gave you permission to beat me to a pulp."

"I would love to, but I'm a McLintock. That's not how I was raised. Bret and Gil's dad taught us how to defend ourselves, but our mother taught us to use physical force as a last resort. Have a seat."

The small office had a desk against the wall on either side and the chairs were back-to-back in the middle. Irving rolled out the one on the right and spun it around. Rance did the same with the one on the left. They faced each other with only a couple of feet between them.

"Okay." Rance swept a hand in Irving's direction. "Talk."

"Did your mother tell you I had a heart attack?"

"Yes."

"It was a bad one. I'm lucky I made it. My dad died from a heart attack when he was a year younger than I am. He was a writer, historical fiction. My grandfather, who also died of a heart attack relatively young, wrote mysteries. My great-grandfather was a newspaper man."

Would have been nice to hear about his literary ancestors before now, wouldn't it? Anger simmered in his belly. Maybe if he'd known he came from a long line of writers he'd have started sooner.

"My father loved that we had this tradition going. He kept hoping one of my kids would show an aptitude so we'd have five generations of writers. Neither of them have any interest at all. He died thinking the line would end with me."

"It did."

"No, it didn't! There's you! I don't know what you're writing, but that's not important. What's important is—"

"That I'm a McLintock."

"Doesn't matter! You're my son!"

"Not in any way that counts." His jaw clenched. "My talent comes from my mother. She nurtured my creativity and fostered my ambition. You don't get to claim *any* of that. Do you hear me?"

"I do. The two of you get all the credit. I don't care what name's on the book."

"Who says there will be a book?"

"Oh, there will be. You just said you have talent and ambition, which means there will be a book, probably several books. Tell me, are any of your siblings writing?"

Damn. He'd said too much. If he refused to answer, that would be an answer. "Not yet."

Irving smiled and folded his hands.

"Doesn't mean what you think it does. They could start any day now."

"You don't want to believe my genes had any part in it, and that's fine. But I'll take comfort in knowing I didn't utterly fail. The chain is not broken, after all."

"Is that the only reason you're here?"

"No, but it's a big part of it. I told myself it didn't matter, but after my heart attack, suddenly it did. And you were my only hope."

"So basically you're here to satisfy your ego needs? To confirm that you passed on your fabulous writing genes to the next generation?"

Irving gazed at him, his brown eyes gleaming with what looked suspiciously like respect. "That would be a bit narcissistic, wouldn't it?"

"It sure as hell would."

"Well, my therapist happens to agree with you. He was against me telling my wife and kids about you, against me coming here and disrupting your family's Christmas."

"I thought therapists were all about confronting your past."

"They usually are, but this guy knows me pretty well by now. I have a borderline personality disorder. At sixty-one, I'm not likely to change."

"Then you really don't care if folks around you get upset. If you hurt them." That was both repulsive and fascinating.

"Not as much as you would. Or your mother. I'm not very emotional. But when I called Desiree to tell her I wanted to come, something weird happened. I started crying. I never cry. It was embarrassing."

"You felt sorry for yourself. Big deal. She told me you cried on the phone. I figured it was an act."

"It wasn't. Something about hearing her voice—"

"Listen, she's happily married, so if you think for one minute—"

"No, no, nothing like that. I enjoy my life. I'll do my best to make this up to my family. I'm not great at apologizing but I'm hoping they'll forgive me. They've put up with me so far."

"Do you want my mother to forgive you?"

"Yes." He looked down at his clasped hands. "I haven't admitted that to myself until now, but I want her forgiveness. I suppose it's an ego thing, too." He glanced up. "And yours, Rance. I want your forgiveness."

To soothe his ego? Not in a million years. "Let me save you some time and effort, Irv, old boy. There's nothing you can do that will make me forgive you for twenty-nine years of silence."

He nodded. "I'll keep that in mind."

30

Lani had promised Desiree she'd participate in the caroling and she prided herself on keeping promises. Her parents had chosen to stay home and be serenaded, so she'd borrowed their truck for the drive over to the ranch house.

The yard in front of the barn bustled with activity. Multicolored Christmas lights decorated Buck's pickup and the railings on the flatbed. She quickly located Rance hauling hay bales and sliding them into position on the trailer floor. Her stomach did a few backflips.

She'd avoid him as much as possible and hope nobody noticed. After pinpointing Sara, she made her way to her sister without crossing his path. "Can I do anything?"

"Not right now. I was standing here waiting for you. The guys have this part under control, Desiree and Marybeth are inside prepping the hot chocolate for later, and Angie's gathering old blankets from the house. We can help her spread them over the bales once she shows up."

"Okay." That might involve interacting with Rance, but she'd handle it. The ball was in his court so she'd fake polite disinterest until he was ready to talk.

Sara handed over some sheet music. "Faye and Gil printed these and I took an extra for you."

"Thanks. I'm rusty on some of the lyrics. I was just gonna go la-la-la."

"That works, too."

"Where's Kieran?"

"Over by the barn practicing the unfamiliar ones with Beau."

"Why? You could teach him."

"Rance and Clint grabbed hay bale duty and Beau was desperate for a job. Kieran mentioned he didn't know all the tunes and Beau immediately offered to fix that problem."

"I don't see Jess and the kids. Or any kids."

"Everybody decided they're too young for something like this. But Jess insisted Beau should be part of it. Mav will love seeing him goof around, which guaranteed he will. But he feels a little lost without them here."

"That's sweet." Thinking of Mav recalled last night's adorable scene — Rance holding her while she waved her baby turtle in his face. Time to focus on something else. "The lights look good on the truck and the flatbed."

"Andy and Sky are trying to connect more strands. Andy wants to make a bigger splash with the lights. Desiree loves 'em."

"So I've gathered. Is that Irving Quick?" She pointed to a tall man wearing a topcoat and a Russian-style furry hat.

"That's him. He keeps trying to strike up conversations with folks and they either ignore him or quickly find a way to escape."

"You'd think he'd take the hint and drive back to town."

"From what I hear, he's on a mission to get Desiree and Rance to forgive him."

"Good luck with that."

"He's also found out Rance has written something, although I don't think he knows what."

"How? I was sure nobody would—"

"He made a good guess and Rance gave it away that he's writing."

"Oh, no." She looked toward the flatbed as the man she adored put down another hay bale and hopped up on the low-slung trailer to shove it into place. "He must hate that."

"I'm sure he does."

"Nothing's working out the way he wanted and now he has to put up with his deadbeat dad."

Sara gave her a sideways hug. "Not your fault, sis."

"I know, but—"

"He had unrealistic expectations."

"And I gave him false hope. Which reminds me. Is Granny here?" She had mixed feelings about seeing Granny. That lady might understand her position, but she also loved Rance and wouldn't like to see him suffering.

"She didn't come. Like Mom and Dad, she decided to stay put and be serenaded. Which is good. If everybody wanted in, we wouldn't all fit on the trailer and we'd have nobody to sing to.

Kieran's looking forward to it. He—oh, damn. Here comes Irving."

"Is there a way we can dodge him?"

"We could say we have to go in the house and help, but he might offer to go with us. Nobody inside would thank us for that."

"Then maybe we can be the most help by keeping him occupied out here."

"That's my thought. Hello, Irving. I don't think you've met my sister Lani."

"Haven't had the pleasure." He thrust out his gloved hand. "That's why I came over."

She shook his hand, glad that she was also wearing gloves, which minimized the contact. She used to be in awe of successful writers, but her job had muted that reaction. For the most part. She'd still be tongue-tied if she ever came face-to-face with Stephen King.

Through her work she'd discovered that writers were just people. She'd never had a reason to actively dislike a famous author.

Until now.

What kind of man fathers a child, abandons him for twenty-nine years and then pops up and makes a pest of himself? Irving Quick's moral compass had to be seriously off-kilter.

But his face — oh, my God — his face was Rance's with thirty years gently added. He was still a handsome devil and his smile was so like Rance's it gave her goosebumps.

"I guess you and I are the outliers."

"We are?"

"The only two who don't live here."

"Oh." She hated being lumped into a category with him but he was correct. "I guess so."

"I hear you're in publishing."

"I am." Chances were good he'd never heard of the company, but she said the name anyway, out of company loyalty. "Square Glasses Press."

He chuckled. "Cute. For Benny Franklin, right?"

"Right." He probably thought calling him *Benny* was clever.

"Sounds like a boutique outfit."

Sara jumped in, bless her. "It's a great company. They have an excellent reputation. Lani's worked with some amazing authors."

"Good editing is so important. I've had some decent editors but inevitably they leave and I have to break in another one."

"How terribly sad for you."

Lani managed to turn her laughter into a cough. Would Irving take offense at Sara's sarcasm?

"You said it. Sad and incredibly frustrating."

Looked like Irving wasn't easily offended.

And he clearly relished having an audience. "You know, I almost envy the writers who skip the traditional route and go indie. Then you get to choose your editor. I think Rance would be smart to take that path."

"Hm." Wouldn't he love that? He might think then he wouldn't have to risk seeing Rance's bestseller sitting in the front of the bookstore, possibly beating out his.

"In fact, Desiree should absolutely consider it, too. She has an editorial board right here. The Wenches could cover edits and Lucky's marketing guru Trent could handle promo. Find a cover artist and she's in business."

And she'd still outsell this stuffed shirt.

"I stopped by L'Amour and More this afternoon. It's charming. The perfect venue for her genre and she can always be assured her books will be in the front window."

"I spent a lot of time in New York before I moved here in the fall." Sara gave Lani a covert nudge. "M.R. Morrison's books are everywhere, including in the front window of bookstores."

He looked like he'd just sucked on a lemon. "Well, yeah. Going indie probably won't change that if she maintains her connections. Anyway, she'd be crazy not to publish her own books, considering she has all this built-in support. I haven't told her so, but I probably will before I leave. She might not have thought of it."

Lani wasn't sure how much longer she could stand there listening to Irving's claptrap. Then Angie came out on the porch loaded down with blankets. "Hey, Sara, Angie's got the—."

"Blankets! Right! Sorry, Irv, we gotta run." Sara wasn't kidding. She race-walked as she headed for the porch.

Lani jogged to catch up with her. "Indie publishing indeed," she muttered.

Sara slowed down. "He's late to the party. Desiree's already thought of it and she may give it a try."

"Huh. She made a reference to it yesterday but I didn't think she was serious."

"Now that she's uncloaked herself, her publisher wants to send her around to bookstores. She'd rather have readers come to her, which is the whole point of the M.R. Morrison tours."

"I can see the appeal, for her anyway. Rance shouldn't go that route, though." She shifted her attention to Angie, who wasn't moving very fast. "That's a big-ass pile of blankets, girlfriend!"

"I won't lie. They're heavier than I expected." She paused to catch her breath as they approached. "Mom's a big fan of wool."

"I thought you'd never come out." Sara relieved her of several. "We got stuck with Irving."

"I'm sorry."

"We survived." Lani took her share and they set off for the flatbed. "That man is a piece of work, though."

"That's what everybody says."

"Oh, and get this," Sara added. "He thinks L'Amour and More is the perfect little venue for your mom's books, a place where she can dominate the front window since she owns the store."

Angie laughed. "Then he's been in there. He must have been shocked to discover that Lucky doesn't have any of his books."

"I think he'd reframe it," Lani said. "Lucky doesn't have his books because they fly off the shelves and Lucky can't keep up with the demand."

Sara nodded. "That sounds about right. So Angie, how did you get along with Adam Bridger?"

"Very charismatic. Mom took to him right away and vice-versa. She and Lucky are stoked about turning a Victorian into a bookshop. Trent's ready to sink his teeth into a new marketing challenge. But if the state doesn't fix that treacherous road, we'd burn a lot of hours going the long way."

"Then I hope they get on that road project. Kieran's *so* excited about working on a Victorian and being part of creating Lucky's third bookshop."

"I could tell. Kendall didn't make it into town to meet Adam, but she's all for it, too, especially if the road gets fixed."

A twinge of envy caught Lani by surprise. Opening a branch of L'Amour and More in an old Victorian sounded like fun, especially because so many family members would be involved. Locally owned bookshops were a passion she shared with the McLintocks.

She couldn't be in the thick of the planning and executing of the new venture, but she'd have to be okay with that. As she'd learned years ago, saying yes to one thing meant saying no to something else.

Or someone else. Saying no to Rance was tough — tougher than anything she'd ever done in her life.

31

Rance sat on a hay bale on the opposite side of the flatbed from Lani. She'd buddied up with Sara, Keiran and Beau, which was good. Originally he'd planned to fake a sore throat to get out of this caroling gig entirely, but he'd made the mistake of telling Granny.

She'd reacted in typical Granny fashion — *Shame on ya, boyo! Ya promised never ta lie ta her again.*

Technically he would have been lying to his mother, but Granny had pointed out that his mom would tell everyone, including Lani, that he had a sore throat, which would result in Lani being lied to, after all.

So here he was, and to make the event extra special, Irving chose to occupy his hay bale. Might have been smart to wait until the guy had taken a seat. Instead he'd prioritized grabbing one the minute Lani had settled on her spot next to Beau. Staying far away from both Lani and Irving had proved to be a tactical impossibility.

"She's stunning."

Rance almost responded with an innocent-sounding *who*. He thought better of it. Irving was a waste of space, but he was also a writer, and writers paid attention. Living with his mother had taught him that.

The crowd was too small and the rift between him and Lani too obvious. Clint had already asked him what the hell was wrong. He'd brushed off the question. Several others had given him funny looks. His mom and Andy, for instance.

Conversation buzzed all around him as Buck put the truck in gear and pulled the flatbed slowly out of the yard. Sky rode with him to help with the tricky logistics of this caper. They'd decided to back the trailer down each narrow lane to put the carolers in range of the folks they were serenading.

They'd lucked out weather-wise, with a crisp clear night and a sky spangled with millions of fairy lights. He'd told Lani a sky like this would renew her belief in Santa. Now he was struggling with his faith in the jolly old elf.

"I've slowly pieced it together." Irving kept his voice down, and the chatter around them provided cover. "You two have a geographical conflict. I doubt you'll be the one and only child to leave Rowdy Ranch and East Coast literary types believe they'll shrivel and die in the wilds of Montana. So I think—"

"With all due respect, I don't give a damn what you think. Please shut the feck up."

"Feck?"

"It's Irish."

"I like it."

"I don't care."

"That's fine. I'll shut the feck up right after I say this one thing. You and your mother should create an indie press."

"Brilliant. Thanks."

"I'm not done. Between the Wenches, two bookstores, Lucky's marketing guy Trent and your mom's experience in the business, she'll do very well and so will you."

"Great. Now would you please—"

"Here's the good part. You need to hire someone to head it up, someone with publishing know-how who would enjoy running her own show."

What the hell? Rance slowly turned his head and looked into eyes exactly like his but with more crinkles around the edges. It was a dumb idea. His mom had only shown vague interest in publishing her own books, Lani wouldn't go for it and he didn't envision starting out that way.

"Like it?"

"Not really. Even if I decided to change my mind about how I'll publish, I doubt my mom's ready to invest time and money in that and Lani doesn't want to change jobs. She loves her co-workers. They have a stimulating environment there."

"Have you been to a Wenches meeting?"

"I snuck in once when I was a kid. Saw most of it before they discovered me and shooed me out. They'll probably want to have me there when they—" Yikes. Irving had fried his brain with this concept. He'd forgotten who he was talking to.

"You've given them your draft, haven't you?"

"None of your business."

"Take her to the meeting. Let her—"

"Listen up, gang," Clint called out. "We're starting with Granny. Rance told me earlier she wants *Grandma Got Run Over by a Reindeer*. She heard the Irish Rovers sing it one Christmas when Kieran took her to Dublin for a concert."

"That I did," Kieran said. "She laughed till she was like to fall over. I'm not surprised she asked for it."

Andy chuckled. "We're not exactly the Irish Rovers. I hope she knows that."

"I told her," Rance said, "and here's her reply. *Yer what I've got and tis glad ta have ya, I am.*" That got a laugh.

"Then I guess we're doing it!" Clint said. "Hang tight until Buck and Sky get us in position. When we stop moving, we'll stand up. Faye's gonna start us off."

Rance heard the instructions but nothing registered. Would anybody notice if he got off here so he could have a heart-to-heart with Granny? Because that's what he needed.

Irving's idea was outrageous and likely self-serving. His mom would laugh at the audacity of it and Lani would just reject it out of hand. He shouldn't even give it space in his head.

Then again, he was desperate. His dream had been jacked from the get-go because he hadn't understood how much Lani cherished her connection to Square Glasses.

Good thing he'd never told her his secret grand plan — that if he moved to a larger publishing house, he'd take her with him. Talk about arrogant. What a deal. She could hitch her wagon to his star. He'd deserved to crash and burn.

This indie concept was also designed to coax her away from a job she loved. Was he despicable because he couldn't stop thinking about it?

She'd told him brainstorming with his mom and Andy had reminded her of discussions at Square Glasses. He had a hunch a Wenches meeting would, too. And her family was here....

Damn it! He'd made a big enough mess as it was. He should probably forget everything Irving had said and—

"Stand up. We're gonna sing."

Irving's soft murmur penetrated the battle being fought in his head. Why was that so? Because Irving's voice was his voice. They sounded the same.

He stood and looked over at his front porch. Granny came out wearing her wool coat and knit hat. She'd found a piece of cardboard somewhere and some markers to make a sign that said *Happy Christmas to My Grand Family!* As she held it up, the smile on her cherubic face was brighter than the lights on the railing.

His throat tightened. Moving to the ranch had been so good for her and life-changing for him. He loved being part of this large brood, but there was a downside, especially since he and Lucky had come as a matched set. He'd had very few one-on-one experiences with someone older and wiser than him. Until Granny.

Faye hummed a note and he did his best to clear his throat and sing. He still sounded like a frog as he launched into the irreverent tune Granny had requested.

She cracked up as Kieran had predicted she would, which cheered him up enough to think that maybe he should at least mention this concept to his mom. If she thought it was crazy, that would be the end of it. But what if she was intrigued?

Irving was no angel come to save Christmas, but his idea had provided a tiny glimmer of hope just when all seemed lost. If it worked — for Lani, her family, his mom, the Wenches — Irving might earn his forgiveness, after all.

32

To say Lani had fun caroling would be a stretch, but she'd enjoyed some highlights. Granny's sign had touched her, and she'd laughed until she was out of breath at Beau's antics when they'd sung *I Want a Hippopotamus for Christmas* to Jess and the kids.

She'd always remember her parents standing on their porch, arms around each other, as the group sang *Silent Night*. They'd had a full life in Trenton, maybe a little too full. Here they were learning to relax. It was beautiful to see.

She envied them a little bit. Their warm smiles had radiated peace and joy. Those emotions weren't within reach for her right now.

She was at odds with the cheerful mood of the carolers as they gathered by the fire in the ranch house living room. She faked it as best she could and vowed to sneak out the moment she could get away with it.

That said, she was dying to know what had sent Rance into a huddle with his mom and Andy. Irving attempted to join their clearly private discussion and was rebuffed. When he started in her direction, she turned her back and dived into a conversation Gil and Faye were having with Beau about what songs to include next year.

Next year. She couldn't even think about it. Rance might have found somebody new. She might have, too, although the prospect of dating made her stomach clench.

"Lani?" Rance's voice, so close, made her jump and twirl around so fast she almost spilled hot chocolate over both of them.

"Sorry. Didn't mean to scare you."

"That's okay." She gulped for air. "I just wasn't…" She met his gaze. "Have you… did you think about…." She couldn't make herself say it. Going to a different publisher was her suggestion and she hated the thought.

"Let's duck into the library."

"Um, okay." She glanced at her mug of hot chocolate. "I should probably—"

"I'll take it." Faye held out her hand.

"Oh." The discussion of caroling choices had screeched to a halt as the three of them gazed at her with great interest. She gave Faye her mug. "Just don't take out *Hippopotamus*. That's a winner."

"They'll take that out over my dead body," Beau said. "And Jess's."

Gil laughed. "I'll be sure and tell her you put her life on the line for that tune."

"Let's go." Rance took her hand.

She shivered as he wove his fingers through hers and led her to the open door of the library. Sam started to follow, but a quick word from Rance sent the collie back to the crowd in the room.

Would this be their last private conversation? He didn't bother to close the door, so he wasn't planning to kiss her. Maybe this was the way they'd say goodbye, surrounded by books. That was appropriate.

The rainbow of wingback chairs formed a semicircle facing the bookshelves that she now knew revolved to create an entrance to Desiree's office. Rance stopped before they reached the chairs. "I have a favor to ask."

She turned to face him as warmth traveled from the clasp of his hand up her arm and through her body. "Of course. I'm happy to be your emissary. I have a good relationship with—"

"This isn't about going to another publisher."

"No? Then what is it about?"

"The Wenches will be discussing my book tomorrow. I'll be there and I'd like you to be there, too."

"Discussing your... they've all read it?"

"Most of them. Mom's contacting each of them now to see if they can manage to finish by two o'clock tomorrow."

"But it's Christmas Eve Day! What's the rush? And don't you have to work?"

"I just checked with Clint and he's agreed to change my hours. I'll be working Christmas Eve, instead."

"But then you can't do the sleigh ride."

"Not necessarily. I might be allowed fifteen minutes to take a spin up and down Main Street."

"Rance, what's going on? I saw you having what looked like a serious talk with your mom and Andy. What happened?"

"They asked why we weren't speaking to each other. I told them."

"All of it?"

"Not all. Just that we've developed strong feelings for each other and as a result you've decided you can't be my editor. And that I... haven't reacted well to that decision."

"What's that got to do with asking the Wenches to gather for a critique on Christmas Eve Day? It makes no sense."

"It will."

"What aren't you telling me?"

His gaze searched hers. "I love you."

Her brain stalled and the air left her lungs.

"Do you believe me?"

She nodded as she struggled to breathe. She'd assumed he did. But hearing the words while drowning in the emotion reflected in his eyes.... that packed a wallop.

"Then please believe this. I want the best for you, even if that means we'll never be together."

She finally found her voice. "Same here."

"I know. I treasure that. And I'm asking you to trust me enough to go along with what sounds like a crazy plan."

She took a deep breath. "All right. It's absolutely nuts, but I'll be here. I'll check to see if I can borrow my folks' truck."

"No need. I'll pick you up at one forty-five."

And she'd lose the ability to get the hell out of there if she wanted to. "I'll find out if there's a problem. If they need the truck, I'll let you know."

"You're afraid to let me be in charge of your transportation?"

"I don't know what I'm getting into."

"Fair enough. After the meeting I'm hoping we can talk. But if, when the meeting's over, you want to go straight home, I promise to take you immediately. No questions asked."

She heard Granny's voice in her head. *He'll do it, luv. He's a man of his word.* "Okay then. I'll see you at one forty-five."

"Thank you." He squeezed her hand and let go. "I'll take a wild guess you'd like to go home now."

"You read my mind. If I go back in there, Irving Quick will be waiting."

"Can I walk you to the front door?"

Her heart melted. "That would be lovely."

He didn't take her hand on the way out and she wanted him to. But she'd restored a boundary when she'd balked at getting a ride over here tomorrow. He was respecting her bid for autonomy.

"Have you told your mom about the changes we made to the manuscript last night?"

"No, ma'am. Didn't mention the Christmas idea, either."

"Why not?"

"I want to see what she and the other Wenches come up with on their own. I don't want them piggybacking on your suggestions."

"I appreciate that."

"After they've had their say, I think you should have yours. If they came up with the same things, you could tell them you've already made those suggestions. But only if you want to."

"Of course I want to. I don't understand why we're fast-tracking this meeting, but I'm thrilled that I'll be able to hear their critiques."

"I'm sure they'll be thrilled to hear yours."

"So why can't we do this after Christmas, since I'll be here until New Year's?"

"I'll tell you after the meeting." He sorted through the coats piled on the coat tree and plucked out hers.

"You really can't tell me now?" As he held her coat, she turned and put her arms in the sleeves. His warm breath caressed her cheek when he settled it on her shoulders.

"I really can't."

His murmured words sent heat spiraling through her body. For one electric moment, she considered asking him to follow her to his cabin. Granny would be asleep by now. He'd probably snap up that suggestion.

But she'd be taking advantage of a man who'd just said he loved her. Turning around, she buttoned her coat and fished the truck keys out of her pocket. "See you tomorrow."

The glow in his dark eyes nearly destroyed her resolve.

Then he reached out and opened the door, letting in a blast of cold air. "Tomorrow."

She stepped outside and the door closed behind her. Hurrying across the porch and down the steps, she paused to glance up at the night sky.

The stars glittered in a dazzling display. That was something she didn't have in Trenton.

She didn't have the scent of evergreens mixed with the aroma of a cedar fire, either. Or a certain cowboy who had captured her heart and wouldn't let go.

She breathed in the crisp cold air of a Montana winter night. "I love you, too, Rance McLintock."

_33_

The Armstrong's yellow truck sat in front of their cabin when Rance pulled in. Lani could have driven herself over, but she hadn't texted to back out of their arrangement. He took that as a good sign.

He'd been getting many of them today. His mom and Andy were on fire with this idea of an indie press. They'd already secured the domain name for DezAndy Press. Trent was designing a website.

Oksana had caught the indie bug and said she'd put out her next book through DezAndy Press. Bret's wife Molly had asked to do book trailers and wanted to take a crack at cover design.

This sea change was happening whether Lani came on board or not. All he could do was cross his fingers and hope.

She stepped out the front door as he climbed down, his boots crunching on a shallow layer of overnight snow that was already starting to freeze. Sunshine was a precious commodity in the winter and only a few hours of it remained on this Christmas Eve Day.

He walked to meet Lani and resisted the impulse to hug her. "You could have driven over, after all."

She held his gaze. "I chose not to."

"I'm glad." He escorted her around to the passenger side and helped her in. "I like driving you around."

She smiled. "I think that's why you bought this truck. To impress the ladies."

"Initially. Until I found the one Thunder liked the best." He closed the door and jogged around to the driver's side. When a sneaky patch of ice almost took him down, he grabbed the fender and saved himself.

He might want to slow down. But damn, he was eager to get to this meeting.

Lani glanced at him as he swung into the driver's seat. "I'm relieved to hear Thunder approves of me."

"Oh, he does." Buckling up, he turned the key and shifted into reverse. "You don't fiddle with the radio, put your feet on the dash or spit out the window."

"Spit out the window? You've had girlfriends who did that?"

He laughed. "No. It was just fun to say. Reminds me of when you wanted me to chew tobacco to mute my sexy factor."

"That was a terrible idea."

"And pointless. My sexy factor can't be muted. It's infinitely resilient."

She grinned. "You're sure in a good mood."

"I am. Which is surprising since I've handed the Wenches my heart on a platter."

"They'll be gentle. They all adore you."

"They all adore Mom, too, but they don't sugarcoat their comments when it comes to evaluating a manuscript. She warned me about that last night. They believe in tough love." Nothing they said would bother him. This meeting wasn't about him. It was about expanding Lani's horizons. Maybe.

"Tough love is what you want from a critique, assuming nobody's on an ego trip."

"They're not. But speaking of egos, have you ever met someone who admits they're a narcissist?"

"Is that what Irving told you?"

"Pretty much. His therapist advised him not to make this trip and he did it anyway."

"Why didn't the therapist want him to come?"

"Because Irving is lousy at apologies — his words, not mine — and he'd only hurt his family and screw up our holiday for nothing." The jury was still out on that. "He says he's a borderline personality who's not likely to change."

"So given all that, why did he come?"

"He's from a long line of writers and his other two kids aren't into it. He figured I might be because of Mom. When I accidently let it slip that I'm writing, he was ecstatic. The chain is still unbroken."

"Is he related to Jeremy Quick, the guy who wrote historical fiction?"

"That's the one. And before that there was a mystery writer."

"Huh. Are you interested in these ancestors?"

"I guess not. I haven't bothered to look them up online." He might, though, once the dust settled.

"Has he suggested you go indie?"

"Yes, as a matter of fact."

"Don't you dare listen to him. He might be happy you're a writer and his precious chain is intact, but he doesn't want to take a chance that you'll eclipse him the way Desiree has."

"I figured out that was his motive."

"And dismissed the idea of going indie, I assume."

"I did. More or less." With an emphasis on *less.*

"More or less? C'mon, Rance. You said you trust my judgment and I predict you'll go far in this business. You have bestseller written all over you."

"Must have happened in the wash. I knew I shouldn't have thrown a dictionary in with my clothes."

"Very funny. Seriously, you have the potential to make the *Times* list, see your books face-out in the front of the store, maybe even get *Tequila Shots* optioned for a movie."

"Sounds exciting."

"It will be. You're a marketer's dream — good-looking, quick with a joke but not full of yourself, and—"

"Don't go overboard, Lani-lou. I seem to recall you telling me to my face that I'm full of myself."

"That was before."

"Before what?" He couldn't resist teasing her. He also wanted to derail this bestseller talk.

She flushed. "Before I saw the real you."

"Naked, you mean."

"Not just that... well, kind of that, but really it was—"

"The mind-blowing orgasms. You can say it. We're totally alone in here."

"Rance! I'm trying to convince you not to listen to Irving. This book combined with your cowboy persona will take you far. You're the whole package."

"I love it when you talk dirty."

"Okay, you don't want to get your hopes up. That's understandable. Publishing's not an easy business, but you have a much better chance than most to make it big. Don't let Irving spook you."

"I promise I won't."

"I take it he's still here?"

"Sure is. He wanted to come to the meeting today but Mom said no and Andy's gonna make sure he doesn't crash it."

"Andy's her knight in shining armor."

"He sure is. He's on guard for all of us, when it comes to that." He parked Thunder beside Nancy's new yellow truck. Once she'd seen what the Armstrongs bought, she'd had to make a change.

Now three Wenches drove vehicles that matched their color. The purple custom paint job on his mom's F-350 was on purpose, but Jess had a green SUV before she was invited to join the group.

Cindy was saving for a metallic blue one and Colleen was determined to find a good deal in red. Teresa said it'd be a cold day in hell when she bought an orange truck. Practical Annette had driven her beige pickup for years and wasn't about to search out an indigo replacement.

He'd known all the Wenches except Jess since he was a baby. And now he was counting on them to save his butt.

Lani waited for him to help her out, which was nice. She kept hold of his hand once she had both feet on the ground. "Are you nervous?"

"A little." But not for the reasons she was thinking. He closed the door and she still didn't let go. Awesome. He tightened his grip and started toward the porch.

"It really is a good book. You must know that on some level."

"I do. But it's like a meal you cook for other people. It tastes fine when you sample it in the kitchen, but the minute they start eating you worry that it's not that great and they'll be too polite to say so."

"But deep down you know it's good, right?"

"Yes, but I know it can be better."

"And that's why we have editors in this world. I don't know if the Wenches consider themselves editors, though."

"Oh, they do. When they read Mom's stuff, they go through it with a fine-tooth comb, looking for plot holes, continuity mistakes and of course, typos."

"That's amazing. If only the authors I work with had something like that."

"The editors at her publishing house always say her manuscripts hardly need anything done to them."

"Do they know about the Wenches?"

"Only that she has a book club. Their true function has always been a secret and I think they'd rather keep it that way."

"Makes sense to me. I'll bet people ask to join."

"They do, and she politely tells them they've capped membership at seven since that's the number of colors in a rainbow."

"Sara told me Jess took her mom's place, which is touching. How long have they been doing this?"

"Mom gathered the group after her first book came out, so almost forty years."

She drew him to a stop at the foot of the steps. "This emergency meeting has something to do with us, doesn't it?"

He hesitated.

"That's my answer. But I can't figure out the connection."

"I'll tell you when it's over."

"I look forward to that."

"Me, too." He'd lay it all on the line and leave it up to her. How would she react? He had no idea.

34

Animated conversation and laughter poured from the library as Rance helped Lani off with her coat and hung it on the rack by the door. She straightened the hem of her Christmas green sweater. It had an applique of Santa and his sleigh in flight.

"Nice sweater."

"I wore it to show you that I support the concept even if I don't take it literally."

"It's only coming up on two o'clock. Plenty of time to change your mind." He gave her a cute little grin.

What an irresistible guy. "If you say so."

"Wait and see." He gestured toward the library. "After you."

When she walked through the door, the energy surrounding her felt familiar — creative people enjoying each other's company. No posturing or pretense, just good fellowship and mutual respect.

The Wenches welcomed her arrival with hugs and favorable remarks about her sweater, which prompted her to check out theirs, which had to match their signature color. They'd all accomplished it, too, even Teresa, whose orange sweater featured Rudolph on the front.

"Good choice," Lani said. "I'll bet it was hard to find."

"*So* hard to find. I used to have an orange one with Santa on it, but all that red clashed something terrible. Rudolph's nose is the only thing that clashes. Big improvement."

"And Rudoph's the hero of the story, after all."

"That's what I say. Way more important than that chubby guy who gets all the publicity."

"I ignored all the Santa-themed outfits and went with Christmas angels." Nancy showed off her yellow long-sleeved shirt that sported a heavenly choir above the words *Joy to the World.*

Desiree's elegant sweater was covered with Christmas ornaments that blended with the purple background. Lani made a note to ask her later where she'd found it.

Colleen and Jess had the easiest task since their colors fit the season. Colleen's red sweater featured Christmas trees and Jess's green shirt portrayed Santa standing beside a brick chimney. Annette's Santa design was like Lani's, except it was set against an indigo twilight sky.

"Alrighty, everybody!" Desiree clapped her hands. "Fashion show's over. Let's take our seats. Rance and Lani, you're up front." She gestured toward two dining chairs facing the semi-circle of wingbacks.

"On the hot seat," Cindy said with a laugh. "Just kidding. We'll be gentle, Rance."

"Not me." Jess gave Rance a smile. "Beau said I should hold your feet to the fire."

"I expect no less." He glanced around the room. "From all of you. No pulling your punches."

"We won't." Annette leaned forward in her chair. "But I was designated to start off this critique by saying that we all agree you've blown us away with this badass book. It's amazing."

He flushed. Adorable. "Wow, thanks. I don't know what to say."

"That's a first," Teresa called out, which made him blush even more.

"Before we give this boy a swelled head, let's address the story's biggest missed opportunity." Nancy gazed at him. "Why set it in November, when you can move the action to December and grab all those tasty Christmas sales?"

Lani blinked. She'd expected comments about pacing and suggested dialogue changes. But Nancy had zeroed in on a marketing issue. The way everyone nodded in agreement confirmed they'd discussed this in advance.

After Nancy broached the subject, the ideas began to flow. A Christmas tree in the bar. A ratty one because Dooley wouldn't bother getting a nice one. Sophia would get rid of it and replace it with something way better. Sophia would try to get him to wear a Santa hat. He'd refuse, then finally do it on Christmas Eve. He was down on Christmas. Why? More ideas about that.

Finally she had to interrupt. "Is anybody writing this down? It's great stuff."

"I am. I'll email both of you with this when we're done.

Lani glanced at Annette. Sure enough, she was typing away on a tablet in her lap.

"But you don't want to overwhelm the core story with holiday references," Colleen said. "That's solid."

"Right, right." Desiree turned in Colleen's direction. "Let's move on to the other major thing."

"Yeah." Annette stopped typing. "Rance, we adore Sophia so much. She's savvy and she's ballsy. And she would have investigated the hell out of Dooley before making a move on him."

Lani sucked in a breath. Holy moly. These ladies rocked.

"I think Lani needs to talk about that." Rance shifted in his seat and gazed at her. "I know we were gonna wait but they need to know we've already worked in the concept."

"By all means," Desiree said. "If you've added something that addresses this, we'd all love to hear it."

"Okay, sure." She quickly outlined the changes they'd made without saying when and where they'd done that edit. But Desiree's thoughtful expression said she'd likely figured it out.

"Oh, and you know what?" Cindy bounced on her chair in excitement, making her red and green ringlets quiver. "I just thought of this. What would bookend Sophia investigating him is if he investigates her later in the book and we find out something we didn't know about her."

"I like it, Cindy." Rance looked over at Annette. "Did you get that?"

"Sure did."

"I loved the book," Teresa said. "I only have one request. Could Dooley have a horse? You have a stable in town. I just think he needs a horse."

"You'd have to find places to work it in." Lani spoke without thinking. "He could—wait, sorry. This isn't my—"

"Go ahead." Desiree gave her a nod.

"Well, he doesn't sleep well, so he sits in the bar thinking about a case, or about Sophia. It might be more interesting if he goes on solitary rides in the wee hours of the night."

"And he sees things," Annette said. "Sometimes significant things."

"And the stable owner is used to him taking his horse out at weird times," Teresa said. "Eventually Sophia finds out. Or doesn't. She might not find out until the next book."

"I could give him a horse." Rance smiled. "I have a bunch to choose from."

Lani hadn't thought of putting a horse in the series but it was brilliant. The lone rider was a Western trope. This session was worth its weight in gold.

Ideas continued to fly around the room and finally Desiree called a halt. "You know what? Let's not have Rance stuff all these good ideas in the first book. He's writing a series. Let's save some for later."

"Like the dog," Colleen said. "Dooley also needs a dog, but not yet."

"Or maybe Sophia needs a dog." Nancy tapped her finger against her chin. "One that doesn't take to Dooley. Dooley has to win him, no *her*, over."

"I'm putting that into a list for future books." Annette typed quickly. "Desiree's right. Maybe the horse should be for later, too."

"No, I want to put the horse in. Unless Lani thinks that's too much."

He'd said it as if she had some authority, but she'd resigned from being his editor. Not a subject to bring up now, though. "I like the horse. I'd say leave that in. It's a great trope."

"And that's a wrap." Desiree stood. "We're at the hour and we've done some great work. Thanks for coming over on short notice."

"No kidding." Rance got to his feet. "I can't thank you all enough. I love the suggestions."

"Thank you all for letting me sit in on a meeting." Lani glanced around as everyone left their chairs. "It's been a privilege. And productive. And fun."

"We loved having you." Annette held up her tablet. "Give me your email so I can send you the notes."

Except she didn't need them. "That's okay. You can send a copy to Rance and he can share them with me... later. He's the one who'll be making the changes."

"Anyone who'd like to stay for a drink is welcome," Desiree said, "but if you need to get home, I understand. It's not like we won't all get together again tonight."

"For the sleigh ride!" Cindy threw her hands in the air. "I can't wait!"

As everyone began filing out of the room, Desiree walked over. "So that's a Wenches meeting. What do you think?"

"You have a fabulous group, Desiree. My brain's still spinning. What a resource you've created."

She smiled. "Co-created. It's a partnership."

"Even better."

"It was terrific, Mom. I knew it would be, but it was even better than I expected."

"Good. I know you've got your shift coming up, but would you like to come sit by the fire for a while?"

"Thanks, but Lani and I will hang in here for a bit. We have some things to discuss."

"Understood. See you both later. Clint's promised me you'll get time to take a sleigh ride tonight."

"Counting on it." He watched Desiree walk out the door and close it. Then he faced her. "So."

"So."

"Want to sit?"

"Should I? Will I need the support for whatever you're about to reveal?"

"I don't know. It's pretty simple. First question, was this Wenches meeting anything like a staff meeting at Square Glasses?"

Her chest tightened. "What if it was?"

"They're the editorial board for a new publishing company called DezAndy Press. It'll be publishing M.R. Morrison, Oksana Jones and... me.

If you'd like to head up that outfit, you have the job."

She stared at him, her ears buzzing. "What have you done?"

"It's not just me. Everybody's excited about it — Lucky, Trent, Mom and Andy—"

She folded her arms and tried to stop from shaking. "This is Irving Quick's doing."

"I'll admit he planted the seed, but—"

"Rance, he's not thinking of *you*. Or your mother! This is all about him eliminating his competition!"

"I don't give a damn what his motives are. He showed me a way that we could be together and I took it."

"You gave up your dream!"

"My dream is you! The *Times* list, books in the front of the store, none of that means anything to me if I can't have you."

"I can't let you do this."

"Lani, I've done it. I'm hoping you'll see how exciting it would be to build this thing together, to make a life together, to have those babies you—"

"You've let a self-involved idiot with half your talent twist your brain into thinking this is your best option. It's not." She clenched her fists, yearning for something or someone to punch.

But not Rance. He'd been talked into sacrificing everything. For her. She knew exactly who she wanted to punch, but this ranch house was a peaceful retreat. And it was Christmas Eve Day. "Please take me home."

"You won't even consider it?"

She shook her head. "I won't be a part of this gigantic mistake."

"Then I'll take you home."

The despair in his voice tore at her heart. "You don't have to do this. Just because your mom and Oksana want to, you can go ahead with your original plan. It's not like you've signed a contract."

He took her by the shoulders. "Look at me."

She lifted her gaze to his.

"Without you, that glittering path you see holds no allure. I don't want some other editor in some other publishing house. If I can't work with you, then I'll work with my family."

She swallowed. "That's your choice."

His grip tightened and his brown eyes blazed. "Come with me, Lani-lou. *Come with me.*"

"No."

The light faded from his eyes. "Okay, then."

_35_

Christmas Eve. Always a magical time at the Buffalo and made even more so with sleigh rides down Main Street. Wagon Train folks came for the ride and stayed for hot cider, both leaded and unleaded, served by the Buffalo's jovial bartenders.

Half the proceeds would go to the charity benefitted by the sleigh ride tickets, a fund to help families regroup and rebuild after a tragedy. It was a worthy cause. On Christmas Eve, Rance donated all his tips to it.

Smiles and jokes tended to increase those tips. He gave it his all, but at this point, his all wasn't worth much. He feared that his smile had turned into a grimace and coming up with funny lines was beyond his reach.

Since news about DezAndy Press and Lani's rejection of running it had spread throughout the family, Clint got the picture early on. His little brother had taken a big swing and struck out.

The last person he wanted to see bellied up to the bar around nine and ordered a hot cider. No telling how Irving had obtained information about his epic fail, but he clearly knew Lani had thrown the offer in his face.

He paid for his cider and added a ginormous tip. "Sorry, kid. Guess she's more entrenched in that world than I thought."

"She blames you." Why even tell him? The guy was oblivious to guilt. And to his credit, he'd partially solved the problem. Publishing through DezAndy Press was far better than Lani hooking him up with some unknown editor back East.

Irving nursed his cider as Rance continued serving other customers. When he raised a finger, Rance got him another cider, took payment and received another outrageous tip.

"I'm giving all my tips to the cause."

"Whatever floats your boat."

"Just thought you should know." He started to walk away.

"Ever read *Gift of the Magi*?"

He paused. "This isn't that story."

"Sure it is. He sells his precious watch to buy a comb for her hair. She sells her hair to buy a chain for his watch."

He shouldn't respond but it ticked him off that the analogy was so off-base. "But in this case, she pitched a fit because she considers the watch priceless and thinks I was gypped out of it by a shyster."

"Did you tell her she was a million times more important to you than the watch?"

"I did. Made no difference. And she rejected my gift, because running DezAndy Press would put her in league with you, the person who ruined my life. No happy ending." He left Irving to his cider.

The next time he glanced in that direction, Irving was gone but Lucky was on his way over. This was ridiculous. He had no time for personal chitchat.

"Hey, Lucky, what can I getcha?"

"Two ciders. Just wanted you to know that Oksana's over in the far corner talking to Lani."

"She's here?" His stupid heart started thumping like crazy and he slopped cider over the edge of the mug.

"Came in with Sara and Kieran. They pretty much guilted her into it. And FYI, Lani told her folks everything."

"Dammit." He overfilled the second one. Wasting product. He never did that.

"Not the intimate details. Calm down. Anyway, Oksana's giving it a shot and talking up the indie angle."

"Tell her thanks. Probably won't work." He cleaned up his mess and handed over the ciders.

"Don't throw in the towel yet, bro." Lucky slapped too much money on the bar and left with the ciders.

Although nothing had changed, Lucky's words lifted his mood a little. Lani was here. Misery loved company. Her Christmas Eve was likely as awful as his.

Would Oksana have any luck when he'd been soundly rejected? Probably not, but it was sweet of her to try.

He'd called his mom before leaving for work and she'd advised him to let it go for now.

Granny had said the same. He'd take the advice of the two wisest women he knew.

Speaking of Granny, was she still here? She'd come in with Buck and Marybeth, who'd promised they wouldn't stay late. But it was now past her bedtime and she hadn't stopped by to say she was going home.

He'd figured she would tell him but she might have come over when he was especially busy and had decided not to bother him. Or in all the excitement she'd forgotten.

That was fine. Tonight was one of the biggest events she'd experienced since she'd arrived here. He'd done his best to minimize the bad news about Lani so she'd have fun instead of worrying about him.

As if his thoughts had conjured her up, there she was, hurrying toward him, cheeks rosy and a bounce in her step.

Climbing up on a bar stool, she leaned forward and motioned him closer. "Come ta have a word with ya, I have."

"You're leaving?"

"Leavin'? I'm just getting' started, I am! They all want me ta ride in the sleigh with 'em! Made at least twenty trips, I have. Tis pure craic!"

That inspired his first real grin of the night. "Awesome."

"Next year I'm dressin' up as Mrs. Santa. Some oul fella says he'll dress as Santa."

"Who's that?"

"Didn't catch his name, but he fancies me."

"I don't doubt it."

She lowered her voice. "Lani's here, lad."

"I know."

"Maybe not fer long." She spoke faster. "Take yer sleigh ride break now. Ask her ta go with ya."

"She'll say no."

"She won't. She wants ta go."

"She told you?" A customer waved at him and he held up a hand in acknowledgment but kept his attention on Granny.

"No. Saw the look on her face, I did. Just do it and don't speak a word about yer troubles. Just put yer arm around her and be quiet. Let her feel the luv between ya."

His throat tightened.

"It'll be alright, boyo." Reaching over, she squeezed his arm, got off the barstool and scurried back to one of the tables.

Peering through the crowd, he caught a brief glimpse of a pudgy older man with white hair and a beard who stood and pulled out a chair for Granny. Well, then.

Next he located Lani in a far corner with Lucky, Oksana, Sara and Kieran. He fetched a drink for the customer who'd waved at him and told Clint he was taking his sleigh ride break. Grabbing his jacket, he made tracks for Lani's table.

She looked wary as he approached and conversation at the table abruptly ended. Granny could be mistaken about this, but he soldiered on, not wasting time on preliminaries. "I'm on a quick sleigh ride break. Would you please go with me?"

She hesitated for what seemed like forever. "Yes, I will."

The collective sigh of relief was almost funny enough to make him smile. Almost.

When she came out from behind the table holding her coat, he helped her on with it in front of their very silent audience of four. Then he held out his hand and she took it. The contact sent arrows straight to his heart.

"Have fun!" Sara called after them as they walked away.

"There's a line." Lani's voice sounded breathy, like she might be short of air, too. "I don't know how long a break you have, but—"

"The Buffalo's staff members get to jump the line. It's our perk for working Christmas Eve."

"That helps."

"Have you taken a ride yet?"

"I wasn't sure I would."

"Worried about sleigh PTSD?"

"You could say that."

"Sorry." He silently cursed himself. Granny had specifically told him to keep his mouth shut. But he had to be a smart-aleck, didn't he?

He paused before taking her past the buffalo. "Look, you don't have to do this."

"I want to."

He met her gaze. "You do? Why?" Then he groaned. "Never mind. Don't tell me. We're going." Was he actively trying to mess this up? Seemed like it. What part of *be quiet* didn't he understand?

Once they were out the door, Sky motioned them to the head of the line where the sleigh stood waiting, having just let off passengers.

As he helped Lani up and climbed in after her, he checked out the two people up on the box.

Then he did a double-take. Harry and Vanessa? And Vanessa was driving?

"Hey, Rance!" Harry turned around and gave him his usual big smile. "Good for you. Lani was making noises like she wouldn't be going on this ride."

Lani adjusted the green lap robe. "It didn't seem fair to take a turn since I'd had the experience the other day and a lot of people haven't had the chance."

"Yes, but you've never had the experience of me driving the sleigh." Vanessa said over her shoulder. "Buckle up, you two."

"Are you taking us on a wild ride, Vanessa?"

She laughed. "No, but it's fun to say that to people. Some look at me and get nervous."

"And the truth is," Harry said, "she's better at this than I am. Buck says she has a gift."

"Thor and I get along." Vanessa made a soft noise with her tongue and the Belgian pulled away from the curb, sending the sleigh bells into motion.

Rance settled back and looked over at Lani, who was gazing straight ahead. He'd made sure to sit down next to her, thigh to thigh, and she hadn't moved away. When he slid his arm around her shoulders, her breath hitched but she didn't glance his way.

Let her feel the luv between ya. He faced forward, too, and concentrated on the good times they'd shared, both in bed and out of it. He relived their first kiss, the phone call after she'd finished the book, dinner with Granny, making love for the first time.

The warmth of her body called to him. He glanced over and her cheeks were pink. Maybe it was the cold, but he didn't think so. She still wanted him. Granny was right about that.

He couldn't ask for a more beautiful setting to charm the woman he loved. The shops on Main Street had outdone themselves this year with garlands, bows and glowing lights.

Last night's gentle snow, gathered in the corners of windows and doorways, sparkled like clusters of diamonds. Even the street glittered as Thor trotted steadily along, his hoofs keeping time with the cheerful jingle of the bells.

At the end of town, where the Christmas tree lot had been until yesterday, Thor made the turn and headed back. Rance didn't want to go back. He could feel the tension slipping away as Lani relaxed against him.

If they could just stay in this sleigh, if he could only kiss her, she'd remember how good they were together. She'd understand why he'd made this decision, why it was the only one to make.

And she'd say yes to a life with him.

<u>36</u>

Lani had never been so conflicted in her life. She knew what Rance was throwing away but he didn't. He'd watched his mother's career unfold, but Desiree hadn't been able to fully embrace her stardom. Hiding behind a male persona had meant no in-person accolades, no media presence, no personal contact with adoring fans.

Rance's talent combine with his dashing cowboy image would captivate readers. He'd end up on a video billboard in Times Square and sell books with his sexy smile. Because those books would deliver on quality, he'd shoot straight to the top.

But none of that would happen because he'd fixated on having her as his editor and couldn't let go of the idea. Irving had capitalized on it to concoct this current scheme.

God help her, she was selfishly tempted to accept the job offer. Working with Desiree, Andy, Oksana, Lucky, Trent and the Wenches would be a blast. She'd be living near her parents and her siblings.

And she'd get the man of her dreams. Rance would star in her professional life and her personal life. She'd have it all... at his expense. How could she make him see that?

Not tonight, for sure. The sleigh ride wasn't the time to debate his choices. Nestled against him as they glided along Main Street had been magical. She'd temporarily let go of the issues between them and soaked up the love.

He had a way of surrounding her with the warmth in his heart. For the length of the ride she allowed herself to sink into that warmth. If he'd drawn her into a kiss, she wouldn't have resisted, even with her mom and dad close at hand.

Her parents hadn't initiated a conversation, as if they'd sensed the emotion of the moment. Her dad would normally have asked Rance how things were going behind the bar tonight. Her mom might have mentioned how pleased she was with the outpouring of support for the charity drive.

Lani counted herself fortunate to have sensitive and observant parents. Sure, they wanted her to move to Rowdy Ranch. If she chose not to, they'd respect that. too.

Thor passed the Buffalo's entrance and made another turn in a parking lot left vacant for that purpose. Lani's mom called out *whoa* and the Belgian came to a halt. The ride was over.

Rance put his mouth close to her ear. "I love you, Lani-lou."

She slowly turned her head. He was close enough to kiss, but putting on a show for the people waiting in line wasn't her style. Or his, thank heavens.

After giving her shoulder a squeeze, he moved the lap robe aside, climbed out and helped her down. Then he thanked her parents for a great ride.

She glanced up at them and managed a smile. "Thanks, guys. Good job."

Her mom smiled back. "Our pleasure, sweetheart. We'll be handing over the reins to Angie and Dallas after one more run. Need a ride home?"

"Yes, please."

"We'll come find you."

"Okay." She turned to Rance. "Thank you for the ride. You'd better get going. I'm sure Clint needs—"

"I'll walk you to your table." He held out his hand.

She took it, grateful for the connection. How often would she hold his hand after tonight? Maybe never. Lovers held hands. But they weren't lovers anymore.

After they passed by the buffalo, setting off his *Meerrrryyy Chriiiistmaaas toooo Yooouuu* message, Rance paused to help her out of her coat and shed his own jacket. "Thanks for going with me."

"I'm glad you asked."

He gazed at her. "Me, too. I—" He stopped himself and shook his head.

"What?"

"Nothing." He took her hand again as he escorted her toward the back table.

Before they made it there, Irving intercepted them. "Lani, I'd like a word. There's something—"

"Please step aside, Irving." Releasing her hand, Rance moved between her and his father. "You've caused enough chaos. She doesn't need—"

"It's okay." She put a hand on his arm. "I have some things I want to say to him." Boy, did she ever. She'd been dying for a chance to rip him a new one.

She wouldn't cause a scene. But before she had to face him over Christmas dinner she wanted to tell him exactly what she thought of his self-serving behavior.

Rance moved with obvious reluctance. "I'll be watching you." He glared at Irving.

His father looked amused. "Oh, to be your age again. I used to be full of fire like that. But that's all in the past."

"Mess with Lani and your future won't look so good, either."

"Understood."

"Lani, if you need anything...."

"I'll let you know. See you tomorrow."

"Right." His jaw flexed. Then he turned away, leaving her with the guy who'd sent the man she loved down the wrong path.

She took a breath. "I hope you're proud of yourself. Rance is now sold on this indie thing when he could have had a huge career. You don't get the enormity of what you've done because you haven't read his book, but—"

"You're right, I haven't read it. But I gather it's damn good from the way his family is buzzing about it. I've also heard that you refused to head up Desiree and Andy's indie press."

"I can't in good conscience be part of it when I know what he could have if he goes the traditional route. I intend to keep making a case for that during the rest of my visit. Maybe I can convince him."

"But Lani, there's something you haven't considered, something that would let you have it all."

"I don't believe you. You bamboozled Rance and now you're trying to do the same with me."

"Hear me out. If you don't agree with my reasoning, then we won't discuss the subject again."

"I'll give you five minutes."

"That's enough. Trust me, these next five minutes could change your life."

<u>37</u>

Rance kept an eye on Lani and Irving. Their conversation didn't last long. Five or six minutes. Shortly after they parted, Lani's parents came in to collect her.

Once she was gone, Rance had to push himself hard to survive until closing. Good thing Thunder knew the way home because he didn't remember much of the drive. Stripping off his clothes, he fell into bed and conked out.

Thump...Thump...Thump. He slowly roused himself and stared into the darkness. What the hell? *Thump.* Then a pause. *Thump.*

His window. Something was hitting it. *Thump.* It almost sounded like... a snowball??? Who would be out there throwing snowballs at his window at... he glanced at his phone... two in the morning? *Thump.*

He turned on a light and struggled into his clothes. The thumping stopped and was soon replaced by a light tap on his front door. Could it possibly be... nah, she wouldn't. Would she?

Running to open it, he came face-to-face with Lani. "Were you throwing snowballs at my window?"

"Yes! I wanted to wake you up but I didn't want to scare you by pounding on your door like it was an emergency. Can I come in?"

"Of course, of course!" He backed up, still dazed and confused. "It's past two in the morning." Like she wouldn't know that.

"I apologize, but I finished your Christmas present and I knew you'd want it right away."

"Pound cake?"

She laughed as she took off her coat and toed off her wet boots. She was wearing the same outfit she'd had on at the Buffalo. But then so was he, minus his socks and boots.

"Not pound cake, but that reminds me. I can pick up the one I made for my folks while I'm here. I was wondering how and when I'd retrieve it."

"How did you get here?"

"I drove their truck. Don't worry, I left them a note and told them where I was going. And why."

"To deliver my Christmas present. At two in the morning."

"Yes. Here." She pulled a folded piece of paper out of her jeans pocket. "It's handwritten because I didn't want to start up my folks' printer in the middle of the night. I didn't wrap it, either, but... it's for Christmas. From me."

He unfolded the paper. *Dear Sasha, I've loved every minute of working with you and the gang at Square Glasses Press, but an exciting opportunity has come my way and I have accepted that offer. We can work out the details at your convenience, but* please consider this my letter of resignation. Sincerely, Atlanta (Lani) Armstrong

He stared at her, his heart doing cartwheels. Could he believe what he'd just read? "Then you're—"

"I'm in!" She flung herself at him. "I'm in, in, in!"

"Oh, my God." He dropped the paper and crushed her against him. "Why? How? What happened?"

Wrapping her arms around his neck, she gazed up at him. "Brace yourself. When I tell you, you'll get mad."

"How can I get mad? You just gave me everything I ever wanted."

"Irving said—"

"Okay, I'm getting mad."

"Let me finish. He said I wasn't considering the big picture and he was right. I hate to admit it, but he pointed out something I hadn't thought of."

"Go on."

"He said you're a born writer who's likely to have a long career."

"That's the goal."

"So it really doesn't matter whether you start out in indie or go the traditional route. If you start out indie and make a big enough splash, the publishers will come to you."

"They will?"

"Not a small press like Square Glasses, which is why I blanked on that concept. We don't have the money. But big publishers pay attention when an indie ebook is selling like hotcakes."

"And then what?"

"They'll make you an offer. Irving said you could work out a print-only deal on books you've already published. They might even offer a publishing contract that appeals to you. In other words, you'd have options. I lost sight of that."

"I'd never make a change if it means I'd lose you as my editor."

"We'll cross that bridge when we get to it."

"I mean it, Lani. I only want your hands on my books."

"How about on your body?"

"Only your hands." He was fully awake, now, especially certain parts of him. "Does this mean you're taking the job?"

"I'm taking the job."

"Wow." He let that miracle settle in. She was taking the job. Moving to Rowdy Ranch. He was grinning and lightheaded, as if he'd just inhaled laughing gas. "By the way, I never got around to telling you there's a stipulation in the contract."

"Oh?"

"You have to marry me."

She smiled. "I knew there had to be a catch."

"There is. I'm it."

"And you're definitely a catch, Rrrance, Rance, Rance." She stroked his cheek. "I accept your terms." Her expression softened and her eyes grew luminous. "Because I love you."

The breath left his lungs. He dragged some back in. "I've waited..." He gulped "I've waited almost a year... to hear you say that."

"Well, get ready, because I'm going to be saying it all the time. You'll get sick of—"

"I won't. I love you so much, Lani-lou."

"And I love you. IloveyouIloveyouIove—"

He laid a finger over her lips.

"See? You're sick of it already."

"Never. But it's kissing time." Lowering his head, he claimed that sassy mouth that had given him some of the worst moments of his life. And some of the most spectacular ones.

He'd gone to bed last night convinced Santa had passed him by this year. Instead, that jolly elf had come through. He'd brought the best gift of all.

* * * * *

Coming February 2025!

**Mosey down the road from
Rowdy Ranch with Montana cowboy
Adam Bridger in an all new
western romance series.**

* * * * *

New York Times bestselling author Vicki Lewis Thompson's love affair with cowboys started with the Lone Ranger, continued through Maverick, and took a turn south of the border with Zorro. She views cowboys as the Western version of knights in shining armor, rugged men who value honor, honesty and hard work. Fortunately for her, she lives in the Arizona desert, where broad-shouldered, lean-hipped cowboys abound. Blessed with such an abundance of inspiration, she only hopes that she can do them justice.

For more information about this prolific author, visit her website and sign up for her newsletter. She loves connecting with readers.

VickiLewisThompson.com

www.ingramcontent.com/pod-product-compliance
Lightning Source LLC
Chambersburg PA
CBHW020403110726
47899CB00006B/1839